MALIFAUX
THIRD EDITION

This text is protected by the copyright laws of the United States of America. Contents copyright © 2005-2019, Wyrd Miniatures, LLC. All rights reserved. This book is a work of fiction; any resemblance to organizations, places, events, or actual persons - living or dead – is purely coincidental. Copies of materials herein are intended solely for your personal, non-commercial use, only if you preserve any associated copyrights, trademarks, or other notices. Wyrd Miniatures, LLC holds exclusive rights to this work. Unauthorized duplication is prohibited. You may not distribute copies to others for a charge or other consideration without prior written consent of the owner of the materials except for review purpose only.

MALIFAUX is a trademark of Wyrd Miniatures, LLC 2005-2019. The Wyrd logo, the MALIFAUX logo, the Through the Breach logo and all related character names, places, and things are trademarks and copyright © 2005-2019 Wyrd Miniatures, LLC. The Malifaux game system is patent pending, serial no. 12/821,427.

CREDITS

CREATIVE DIRECTION
Nathan Caroland & Eric Johns

PRODUCER
Kelly Brumley

DESIGN
Matt Carter, Mason Crawford, & Kyle Rowan

ADDITIONAL DESIGN
Aaron Darland

WRITING & EDITING
Mason Crawford & Kyle Rowan

GRAPHIC DESIGN & LAYOUT
John Cason

ART
Lino Drieghe, Hardy Fowler, Sarah Lindstrom, Christophe Madura, & Alyssa Menold

SPECIAL THANKS
Tim Akers, Owen Beste, Rafał Bieliński, John Biffle, Kyle Bode, Neil Brown, Kimberly Cooper, Jordon Davis, James Doxey, Jason Fryer, Philip Hawtin, Kai Hull, Samantha Joelsson, Matt Lewin, DZ Liergaard, Nathan Linder, Sean Overton, Craig Shipman, Jamie Varney, Brad Vender, Mike Wallace

And a particularly special thank you to all of our amazing Alpha, Closed Beta, and Open Beta playtesters, as well as our volunteers and Henchman all around the world! Thanks for keeping it Wyrd.

TABLE OF CONTENTS

THE FACTIONS OF MALIFAUX 2
THE HISTORY OF MALIFAUX 4
  Old Malifaux 4
  Hidden Pathways 7
  The Present 31
MAP OF MALIFAUX 34
MAP OF MALIFAUX CITY 36
HOW TO PLAY 38
  What You Will Need 38
  What Makes Malifaux Special? 39

Components 40
  Models 40
  Stat Cards 40
  Upgrade Cards 42
  Fate Cards 43
  Using the Cards 44
  Duels 46
  Triggers 48

The Table 49
  Measuring 49
  Moving 50
  Line of Sight 52

Gameplay 56
  Start Phase 56
  Activation Phase 57
  End Phase 57
  Actions 58
  Resolving Actions 59
  Abilities 60
  Damage 60
  Friendly, Enemy, & Control 62
  Engagement 62
  Soulstones 63
  Tokens 63
  Markers 64
  Conditions 65
  Area Effects 66
  Math 67
  Replace 68
  Summoning 68
  Bury 69
  "Once Per" Effects 69

"This or That" Choices 69
Timing 70
Sequential Effects 70
Actions Generated by Effects 70
Detailed Timing 71

Terrain 72
  Cover & Concealment 72

Encounters 76
  Encounter Setup 76
  Gameplay 79
  End of Encounter 79

Strategies 80
  Turf War (⚙) 80
  Plant Explosives (📖) 80
  Corrupted Idols (🐾) 81
  Reckoning (✗) 81

Schemes 82
  1. Detonate Charges 82
  2. Breakthrough 82
  3. Harness the Ley Line 82
  4. Search the Ruins 82
  5. Dig Their Graves 82
  6. Hold Up Their Forces 82
  7. Take Prisoner 82
  8. Power Ritual 83
  9. Outflank 83
  10. Assassinate 83
  11. Deliver a Message 83
  12. Claim Jump 83
  13. Vendetta 83

INDEX 84

THE FACTIONS OF MALIFAUX

THE GUILD

The Guild of Mercantilers is often seen as an omnipresent, ever-vigilant force that protects citizens against criminals and the monsters that roam Malifaux. What few people realize is that this strength is a carefully maintained illusion. Protection of the people is a secondary motivation at best; their interests lie only in Soulstones, and each shipment sent back to Earth helps solidify their stranglehold over the world's most powerful nations.

THE ARCANISTS

A secretive branch to the Miners and Steamfitters Union, the Arcanists believe that humans should be given free rein to embrace magic and revel in its power. To outsiders of the organization, they are seen as anarchists and criminals, but to those who share their vision, the Arcanists are an ambitious collection of everyday working men and spellcasters that are capable of truly wondrous feats.

THE NEVERBORN

The creatures that humanity has dubbed the Neverborn are the native inhabitants of Malifaux. Some are the twisted descendants of the world's original occupants, while others are nightmarish ghouls created through bizarre spells or magically-enhanced evolution. Many Neverborn believe that humanity is a scourge that must be cleansed, but those rare few believe that they have an important role in this world's greater schemes. Only time will tell.

THE FACTIONS OF MALIFAUX

THE RESURRECTIONISTS

A loose cabal of necromancers, grave robbers, and cold-hearted killers, the Resurrectionists have a mutual animosity for the Guild and any that would deny them their morbid curiosities. Drawing upon the unnatural power of the Grave Spirit, these necromancers invoke dark miracles that shake the very balance of life and death and populate the abandoned districts of Malifaux City with shambling undead.

THE TEN THUNDERS

Dabbling in assassinations, blackmail, racketeering, burglary, gambling, kidnapping, smuggling, drug trafficking, and anything else deemed illegal, the Ten Thunders is a crime syndicate primarily based in Malifaux City's Little Kingdom. Sworn to secrecy and expected to willingly give their lives for the organization, members are exceedingly devoted to their cause, which is to ultimately gain control of Malifaux in its entirety.

THE OUTCASTS

These hardy men and women are those who seek out an existence free of law and oversight of the Guild and their ilk. The Outcasts often make their way as scoundrels or mercenaries, selling their services to the highest bidder. Often rubbing elbows with those in power, these guns-for-hire take on the dirty tasks others would avoid... or seek their own paths to power.

THE BAYOU

Nestled to the east of Malifaux City is the Bayou, an expansive swamp with open marshes, flooded wetlands, and acres of pig farms. Beneath the branches is a cobbled-together Gremlin society that mimics the important elements of humanity, like brewing alcohol, shooting guns, and generally being a lethal nuisance to society. The Bayou is a chaotic place, and the denizens will do whatever it takes to keep it that way.

THE EXPLORER'S SOCIETY

Originally established as a means to reinvigorate the long-dulled sense of adventure of its founder, the Explorer's Society has since expanded to focus on unfurling the mysteries of Malifaux and beyond. These aristocrats, dark tourists, and pioneers venture into the unknown corners of this world to seek knowledge, discover new locations, and hunt big game. While their motivations are unclear, their recent push to amass rare artifacts is not.

THE HISTORY OF MALIFAUX

Malifaux is a world set aside from our own. Located in another realm, in another dimension of reality, it is home to monsters and mankind alike. Far too often, the two become indistinguishable from each other.

Despite being a different world, Malifaux is similar to Earth in many ways. It has breathable air, discernible seasons, and a blue sky with a sun that rises in the morning and sets in the evening. The soil is suitable for growing crops, and Earth plants have been successfully transplanted to Malifaux (and vice versa) with few issues.

Though there are differences. The stars and constellations in the night sky are completely different from those of Earth, and two moons - the bright Illios and the darker Delios - hang overhead at night. Some people claim that the sun makes colors appear brighter and more vivid in Malifaux, as if the world had been painted onto glass, but the majority of people who travel to Malifaux don't notice that much of a change.

In short, Malifaux may seem strange, and it's certainly dangerous in the way of untamed wildernesses, but it's rarely *alien*. Most natural laws, as humanity understands them, continue to function on Malifaux just as they do on Earth.

The one notable difference that separates Earth from Malifaux is the abundance of magical energy. On Earth, spellcasters have always had to struggle to draw upon the magical energy; only the most powerful spellcasters, emboldened by mystical runes and arcane phrases passed down since ancient times, could even hope to harness this mystical power.

In contrast, Malifaux is saturated with magical energy. The same arcane words that could barely light a candle back on Earth are enough to summon up a whirlwind of fire in Malifaux, and even those with no talent for magic gradually find themselves developing strange abilities as the latent magic of the world seeps into their bodies and souls.

The true history of Malifaux is lost to the annals of time. There are truths and deceptions buried in equal measure among the legends told by its native denizens, but humanity has been able to piece together these myths to create a plausible idea of what Malifaux was like prior to the opening of the Great Breach.

OLD MALIFAUX

Long ago, Malifaux was inhabited by people similar to humanity. They loved and fought each other as humanity does, creating items of beauty and weapons of war in equal measure. Their earliest civilizations learned of magic and studied its use, and as one empire crumbled to make way for the next, magic and technology advanced in tandem with each other.

In time, the people came to believe that they were masters of magic and technology. They believed that they could solve any problem, rise to any challenge, and one by one, they solved the greatest problems that plagued them:

THE HISTORY OF MALIFAUX

poverty, disease, sickness, pain... Eventually, the most clever among them found ways to live without end and ushered in an era of peace and prosperity.

Gradually, however, these visionaries grew bored with their long lives and sought out ways to keep themselves entertained. Some created breathtaking art that pushed the boundaries of the senses, some set out to gather the knowledge of their people in order to share it freely with their brethren, and others delved deeply into hitherto unexplored realms of magic. Others altered their bodies and the bodies of those around them in ways they found pleasurable, creating new races through advanced science and magical ritual.

The Tyrant War

A handful of the bored immortals turned their attention toward darker pursuits. They found dangerous ways to waste their time, and mastered each one in turn.

What was a thrilling dip into the dark waters for some became a headlong, breathless plunge into depravity for others. They found deep within themselves the worst perversions and most terrible desires, and knowing no limits, they turned these things outward onto their fellows. They reveled in the misery they caused and subjected their kin to cruel experiments and unspeakable sadism simply for their own amusement and edification. Illness and pain once again abounded in Malifaux.

Drunk on their own power, these entities cast aside their mortal names and souls like snakes shedding their skins... or perhaps, like moths emerging from cocoons. They assumed sobriquets to describe their new selves - Plague, Obliteration, Meridion, Despair - but to those who had not ascended, there was only one word to describe what they had become: Tyrants.

These Tyrants were so powerful that they seemed as gods. The desperate people of Malifaux exhausted every available force to stop the Tyrants. They turned to new magic and explored technologies that had previously been too dangerous to consider. Terrible creatures were created through magical rituals and spawned in chemical vats to be unleashed upon the Tyrants in the hope of exploiting an unknown weakness. Armies the likes of which the world had never known marched in the shadows of terrible, world-shattering war machines.

Despite the best attempts of Malifaux's people, however, nothing seemed capable of standing against the potency of a Tyrant's magic or their mastery of the sciences. The great machines of war were swept aside like children's toys, and entire armies were slaughtered in the blink of an eye.

Titania's Bargain

When all seemed lost, it was the queen of the people who rekindled the hope of victory. Titania gathered the scattered warriors, artificers, and mystics to her side and told them of her dreams and the machine she saw there. The machine, she claimed, would allow her to harness the power of death itself in order to destroy the Tyrants once and for all. The glimmer of hope was all that the survivors needed, and they turned all of their efforts toward the creation of Titania's Kythera device.

THE HISTORY OF MALIFAUX

Unbeknownst to Titania's followers, she had betrayed them. The Kythera device was not designed to merely channel the power of death, but rather, to bring the personification of death itself - the Grave Spirit - into Malifaux; Kythera was a dimensional portal. As it began to open, the Grave Spirit completed its end of the bargain and infused Titania with its fell power. Only then did her subjects finally realize the full extent of the dark bargains Titania had made with the entity.

As their queen turned the power of the Grave Spirit toward the Tyrants, killing their physical bodies, the people who had built Kythera worked desperately to undo what had been done. In the end, they proved unable to close the device, but they did stop the portal from opening any further than it had. The corruptive, necromantic power of the Grave Spirit was seeping out of the device, but the entity itself had been prevented from crossing over and devouring all life in Malifaux.

The act of channeling so much necromantic power had killed Titania, but rather than dying, she passed into undeath and became a sentient, walking corpse. She expected admiration for defeating the Tyrants, but her subjects had seen what she had nearly unleashed upon the world and turned on her.

Undead had never existed in Malifaux before Titania, and her former subjects were concerned that executing her might release her corrupted soul, transforming her into a far greater threat. Instead, they altered the plans for Kythera and built a second structure - Nythera - to serve as a prison for Titania and those members of her court who were still loyal to her. It was believed that Nythera would keep her contained for all time.

The Great Binding

In the decades that followed the end of the Tyrant War, the survivors gradually began to realize that the Tyrants had not been entirely defeated. Their physical forms had been shattered, but their spirits had endured Titania's assault and lingered in the aether as specters of their former selves. Though relatively powerless in this ethereal form, the Tyrants could still exert their will upon the world in a limited manner.

Worse yet, they seemed capable of forming spiritual bonds with mortals, granting that mortal power as the Tyrant gradually consumed their soul and took their place in the world. Fearing the return of such powerful enemies, the people of Malifaux turned their attention toward trapping the Tyrants in magical prisons. The prisons varied in form and function, utilizing whatever worked best to bind each Tyrant's power.

Many of the Tyrants had their own power turned against them. Meridion drew her power from the ley lines that crisscrossed the world, so the survivors imprisoned her within them, forcing her to destroy the very power that gave her strength in order to escape. Obliteration's power stemmed from its ability to manipulate time and remove things from reality, so its jailers constructed its prison from the Tyrant's own spiritual form, ensuring that any act of escape would be tantamount to suicide.

Other Tyrants were too subtle or powerful to be bound in such ways, necessitating the need for cruder prisons. Plague was bound within the Necropolis beneath Malifaux City and warded with spells that would turn aside anything approaching, Cherufe was imprisoned in a cage high in the sky, where its flames sputtered and died without fuel, and Despair was sealed inside a fiendishly clever puzzle box.

One by one, each of the Tyrants was bound in prisons crafted from their own power. Some realized what was happening and chose to exile themselves to different realms of reality: Nytemare fled to the dream world, for instance, while the Dragon split its essence in half, leaving part of itself in Malifaux as it flung its other self through the dimensions and into another world entirely... Earth.

The passage between dimensions greatly weakened both that portion of the Dragon's soul and the barrier that separated Malifaux from Earth, though it would be millennia before the full ramifications of that weakening would be felt.

The Twisting

The people of Malifaux had won the war against the Tyrants and bound their spirits, but the price they paid for their victory was steep. The Tyrants had used their magic and science to twist the minds and bodies of their servants and enemies into useful tools, and now, the monstrous survivors of those experiments struggled to find a place in the world.

Some of these creatures, such as the Nephilim, turned their backs on their former masters and took to hunting down those who still served the Tyrants. Others turned to whatever fragments of magic they had scavenged from the fallen Tyrants, using it to mutate their forms into new shapes that their vengeful brethren would not recognize.

Gradually, the survivors of the war began to drift away from each other. The great cities - the sites associated so strongly with the Tyrants - were shunned as the people migrated into the wilds. With each generation, the trappings of civilization fell further away until the people had regressed into tribes and packs.

Distracted as they were by the aftermath of the Tyrant War, the survivors failed to realize that a far more insidious threat was growing in their midst. The Kythera device provided a link between Malifaux and the realm of the Grave Spirit, and its corruption gradually spread outwards from the portal, transforming the land and poisoning the minds of those who had survived the war. Those who had settled in the most heavily affected areas turned once again to the magic of the Tyrants, reworking their bodies into forms that could survive the spreading corruption.

Centuries passed, and with each generation, the various transmutative magics that had been worked upon the people seeped into their offspring and their offspring's offspring, until eventually, every one of their descendants possessed an ability to change its physical form. For many, this change became a fixed part of their growth cycle, such as with the Nephilim, who required red blood to grow larger, but others retained a greater control over their forms and learned how to change their appearance on a whim.

HIDDEN PATHWAYS

The Dragon was the first entity to travel from Malifaux to Earth, but it was not the last. The fissure caused by its flight was unstable, and through the centuries, portals occasionally opened up between Earth and Malifaux, joining the two worlds for a short time.

The Falling Star (6000 BC)

The half of the Dragon that had been tossed between dimensions appeared on Earth near Mount Etna on the island of Sicily. The Tyrant's arrival triggered a massive volcanic landslide that caused a megatsunami, devastating the eastern Mediterranean coastline on the continents of Europe, Africa, and Asia. Weakened by its travel through the dimensions and trapped in a world with far less magical power than Malifaux, the Dragon settled within the mountain's searing core to slowly regain its strength.

In the years that followed, the people of nearby Crete realized that symbols and icons bearing snake motifs had become infused with weak healing powers and began using such icons to ward their homes and heal the sick.

Journey East (5400 BC)

Following rumors and legend, a Cretan shaman traveled to Sicily in the hopes of finding the source of the healing power her people believed resided within Mount Etna. She succeeded in discovering the spectral form of the Tyrant, which promptly possessed her and forced her to do its will. Believing that she had been chosen by the gods, the shaman traveled eastward as the Tyrant directed her from one land to the next, devouring whatever scraps of power it could find in order to regain its strength.

Though kept strong and youthful by the Dragon's influence, the shaman's body eventually failed her and she collapsed into a river in what would one day become Tibet. The Dragon found, to its horror, that it could not separate itself from its host's corpse, and millennia slowly passed as the Tyrant struggled helplessly within its cage of water and bone.

Blood of My Blood (500 BC)

While hunting, a Native American hunting party came across a group of six Malifaux natives in what would one day become modern day Ohio. The hunters were confused by the strange-looking people they found and the incomprehensible language they spoke, but they took pity on the refugees and brought them back to their camp.

Over time, the natives of Malifaux learned the language of the hunters and took spouses from among the tribe, eventually birthing the first children who were the products of two different worlds. These men and women became known for their ability to run with the wolves or fly with the crows, a gift that they passed on to their children and grandchildren.

The descendants of those original hunters eventually split and went their separate ways, spreading their magic-infused bloodline throughout the native people of North America. The ability to shift shapes and walk with animals grew weaker with each subsequent generation, until they were only myths and legends, but in every generation, there were a handful of people with a stronger connection to their heritage.

The Living Forest (220 AD)

A short time after the turn of the millennium, a portal opened deep within the Amazon rainforest, allowing a small group of plant spirits known as Waldgeist to wander curiously onto Earth. Undisturbed by this occurrence, the plant spirits began exploring their new home and communing with the surrounding trees.

THE HISTORY OF MALIFAUX

Over the next millennia, the number of indigenous tribes living with the rainforest plummeted noticeably as the tree spirits and their offspring fought back against what they perceived as trespassers in their lands. Eventually, stories of its dangerous plant life would reach as far as northern Europe and eastern Asia, though few truly believed the strange stories coming from such an "uncivilized" land.

The Rise of the Dragon (770 AD)

The Indian monk Santaraksita attempted to build a monastery beside a Tibetan river, but each time, the river surged upwards, knocking the temple back down. Terrified, the workers began to whisper of a demon hiding in the river and refused to have anything further to do with the temple.

Fearing for the well-being of the nearby populace, Santaraksita sent for his fellow monk, Padmasambhava, to help him banish the demon and purify the construction site. Instead, the two monks encountered the Dragon, which leapt from the bone fragments of the Cretan shaman and into Santaraksita.

Padmasambhava immediately realized that Santaraksita had been possessed by a spirit far more powerful than he could imagine. Bowing low, the monk approached the Dragon cautiously, giving it the respect he believed it deserved. Padmasambhava appealed to the Dragon's ego and, after a long conversation that stretched across three days, convinced the Tyrant that the wisdom of Buddhism would hold more answers to its plight than wanton destruction. The Dragon listened to the monk, but in its mind, it was already considering what would happen when its current host perished. None of the workers had been suitable hosts; only the monk had the spiritual fortitude necessary to house its essence. In the end, the Dragon agreed to allow the temple to be built, not out of altruism, but out of self-interest.

The Dragon spent the next few centuries wandering Tibet, gathering the wisest humans it could find and either bringing them back to its temple at Samye or inspiring them to build more temples that could house its greatness. Gradually, it twisted the tenets of Buddhism to fit its own needs, creating a dogma that had but one purpose: to prepare humans to become the Dragon's next host.

It would take countless millennia to amass enough magical power to ascend in the starved world of Earth, but the Dragon was patient and had ensured that when its host finally perished, it would have another ready to assume the honor of bearing its spectral essence.

The Masamune Nihonto (1293 AD)

Back in Malifaux, a shaman with delusions of ruling over its people freed a powerful spirit from the magical wards that bound it. As the last of the binding enchantments fell away, the spirit revealed itself to be the Tyrant Shez'uul and possessed its horrified savior.

Shez'uul's host was unsuited for such a potent spirit and began to fall apart almost immediately. The Tyrant was powerful, however, and it supplemented its host's life with the blood of those it killed, gradually transforming its unwitting host into a creature of flowing blood. The scattered tribes of Malifaux were forced to unite against the weakened Tyrant.

In the end, the Nephilim turned the tide of the battle by undergoing a ritual that transformed their blood into a corrosive black ichor that proved to be catastrophically destructive to the red blood making up the Tyrant's borrowed form. Rather than allow itself to be bound once more, the Tyrant used what remained of the power it had gathered to hurl itself through the dimensions, much as the Dragon had once done.

The weakened Tyrant appeared in the Kanagawa Prefecture of Japan, triggering a mighty earthquake that devastated the city of Kamakura and killed tens of thousands. Realizing that it had barely survived the journey between dimensions, the Tyrant bound its fraying and ragged essence to a samurai lord and forced the man to slaughter those under his command to supply the Tyrant with their blood.

As the body count climbed higher and higher, a desperate prefect traveled into the mountains to petition the master swordsmith, Goro Nyudo Masamune, for assistance. Masamune gave the greatest of his blades, the Masamune Nihonto, to the prefect, who used it to cut away and imprison the evil spirit that had possessed his lord.

The prefect enshrined the sword in his home, where it rested until it was stolen forty years later during the Genko War. The blade passed into legend as Shez'uul influenced its wielders, subtly pushing them toward greater acts of bloodshed and violence, which the Tyrant fed upon like a starving prisoner.

Glimpses of Huitzilopochtli (1332 AD)

In the fourteenth century, a portal between Earth and Malifaux opened in the Valley of Mexico, unleashing burned and twisted monsters onto the outskirts of Tenochtitlan. The Aztecs were unprepared for the sudden appearance of these creatures, and the glimpse they received of another world - of blasted plains that had been scorched during the Tyrant War and the titanic, charred beasts that lumbered through the flames - shook their civilization to the core.

Once the portal had closed and the screeching beasts had been slain or driven off, the Aztec people struggled to interpret what they had seen. Many of the creatures they glimpsed were folded into their religion, becoming gods and deities. They believed that the world they had seen through the portal - Malifaux - was a vision of the future after the sun had perished, and in an attempt to avert this perceived fate, their beliefs led the Aztec people down a dark, bloody path.

Spurred onward by their "visions," the Aztec became more warlike and aggressive. Over the next hundred years, they came to dominate the Valley of Mexico and its surrounding areas. Human sacrifice was not unknown before the Aztecs, but they took the practice to an unprecedented level, at one point sacrificing over eighty thousand prisoners over the course of four days.

This was done in the belief that the blood and beating hearts of the sacrifices would empower their sun deity, Huitzilopochtli, with enough strength to continue fighting against the "monsters" that beset him. If Huitzilopochtli failed, the Aztecs believed, then they would perish as well, for there would be nobody to stand between them and the horrors they had witnessed.

The Fury of Horomatangi (1575 AD)

In the later half of the sixteenth century, the Maori of New Zealand witnessed a portal opening a hundred feet in the air above the ocean. The portal unleashed a deluge of water that poured down from the sky like a waterfall, bringing dozens of strange Malifaux fish to Earth. Unfortunately, the great Horomatangi, an ancient and titanic sea beast that had fought for Meridion during the Tyrant War, was also pulled into Earth's oceans by the resulting current.

Horomatangi proceeded to terrorize the people of New Zealand for the better part of fifty years, feasting on the Maori whenever they went to hunt or fish. The great beast was eventually defeated by the efforts of the Ngaatoro sisters, two women who adorned themselves with poison and tricked Horomatangi into devouring them. The poison did not kill the great monster, but it did weaken Horomatangi enough to send it into a deep sleep, winning peace for the Maori people and cementing the Ngaatoro sisters as guardians of the island.

An Empire of Miracles (1642 AD)

In the seventeenth century, another portal opened in eastern Africa, in the nation of Abyssinia. No monsters poured forth from the dimensional rift, and in their curiosity, the Abyssinians explored the seemingly desolate new world and discovered a cache of Soulstones.

The Soulstones were brought through the Breach in the belief that they were normal gemstones, but it was only after the portal closed that the true properties of the Soulstones were realized. When someone died near a Soulstone, the gem would become charged with magical energy which could then be used to cast spells of incredible power.

In the wake of their discovery, Abyssinia became known as a strange and mystical place whose people could wield terrible magical powers. Over time, however, the owners of these Soulstones fought with one another, and the gemstones that fueled their incredible power were gradually lost or destroyed.

Eventually, the number of Soulstones grew so few that the mystical reputation of Abyssinia faded into legend, and they became just another nation, albeit one with unusually advanced cities and some odd traditions.

The Formation of the Council (1780 AD)

Gradually, the spellcasters, shamans, mystics, and healers realized that the meager magic of Earth was dwindling. There were many theories on why the incantations and rituals that had worked for so long were becoming less and less effective with each passing year. Some believed it to be a natural cycle, a tide of magic that would ebb with time. Others thought that there might be a conflict between magic and science, that the growing industrialization of the world might somehow be smothering the arcane rules of magic beneath the spreading influence of science.

The sorcerers, warlocks, soothsayers, and wizards of the world gradually came together to search for a new source of magic. Calling themselves the Council, the group traveled the world in search of a way to replenish Earth's magic. Their members traveled to the New World to speak with the shamans of the indigenous tribes and to eastern Africa to investigate rumors of their powerful sorcery.

At every turn, they found mystics who had noticed the decline of magic but had no answers to give them.

Eventually, the Council began to realize that there was a world beyond their own, and that much of Earth's

THE HISTORY OF MALIFAUX

magic could be traced back to encounters with that hidden world. Only the faintest of dimensional walls kept the two worlds apart... and with enough force, any wall could be knocked down.

The Great Breach (1787 AD)

It took years of research and cooperation, but the Council came to believe that they possessed the magical power necessary to breach the veil between their world and the next. A great call was sent out across the Earth, passed from cabal to secret society to coven, asking anyone with even a shred of magical talent to gather at Santa Fe, in North America.

From all corners of the Earth and from all walks of life they came, the last of their kind. Hoary, bearded sages from the Siberian steppes, Abyssinian artificers, bespectacled Parisian demon worshipers, stoic Indian gurus, ancient Romani crones, far eastern souleaters, and wizened viziers from the Ottoman Empire, all converged on Santa Fe in one final, desperate gambit: a ritual to ensure that magical power was not forever lost from the world.

When the Council's leaders agreed that it was time, they called the entire city into position. The streets teemed with sorcerers and wizards at every junction, each prepared to do their part in the most powerful spell ever cast.

The ritual was grueling beyond imagining. For a day and a night, the hundreds of gathered practitioners poured their last remaining magic into the growing spell. Some were overcome and perished from the strain of it, while others willingly relinquished the last of their life's essence in a final act of desperate sacrifice. The mages who participated were later unable to agree whether the ritual succeeded or failed, but the results were impossible to ignore.

As the ritual reached its zenith, the life force of the lesser sorcerers was torn from their flesh in a torrent of pain and power as the energies of the ritual raced out of control and consumed them. The sudden change in atmospheric pressure combined with the dangerous amounts of gathered aetheric energy to produce a massive shockwave that knocked the largest buildings to the ground while ripping the smaller structures from their very foundations.

In a single moment, Santa Fe was reduced from a thriving settlement to naught but ruin, insanity, and corpses. The city was gone, replaced with a ragged hole in existence and a scant few sorcerers and mystics who were shielded from the worst of the blast.

In the days and weeks to come, the few survivors found that their magical aptitudes had increased exponentially and that unimaginable power now coursed through their veins. Feats of aetheric manipulation that would have taken an archmagus numerous lifetimes to achieve were suddenly at their beck and call. The most powerful magi, conjurers, and shamans the world had ever seen crawled free of the ruins that had once been Santa Fe and peered through the dimensional rift that would come to be known as the Great Breach.

On the other side of the Breach, the surviving members of the Council found a city. Its features were both familiar and strange, as if all the great cities of Earth history had been stacked and shuffled. The buildings leaned and loomed over the streets, and unknown writing was carved in the stone or painted on doors. A sign hung above the city's shattered gates, bearing a word that they took as the name of the city and world alike: Malifaux.

Tentatively, knowing that the new Breach could collapse at any moment, the Council began to explore the city. Old tomes and artifacts littered the ground, and when they realized the power held by these arcane items, the sorcerers snatched them up as quickly as possible. Though joined by a common goal, the members of the Council had little in common with each other beyond their talent with magic, and soon tempers flared as magi and sages accused shamans and gurus of hoarding magical knowledge they believed should belong to them all.

By the end of the first night, these conflicts had erupted into outright warfare. Balls of fire, lances of ice, and bolts of lightning were hurled across the streets and into the sky as the mages attempted to steal the power of their peers or defend whatever magical relics they had claimed for themselves. Friend fought friend, and bitter rivals became desperate allies.

After a fortnight of intense battle, the mages began to gather together into cabals for their own protection, though others were driven northward toward the distant mountains or back through the Breach to Earth. Eventually, one faction succeeded in executing the last of their rivals and seized control of the city. The Council had been reborn.

Early Exploration

In all of their feuding, the Council's mages had not seen any sign of sentient life within the city other than themselves. The sheer size of the city made any sort of exploration difficult, however, and grudgingly, the Council retreated back to Earth to solidify their control over the portal.

A veritable army of mercenaries was chartered to ensure that the Breach was defended against anything that might come through from the other world. Small groups of explorers were enlisted to begin investigating the old city and its surroundings, and academics and archaeologists by the score were gradually brought to the ruins of Santa Fe to begin unraveling the city's mysteries.

Everyone brought to explore the new world was hired with great secrecy. They spread rumors of a terrible earthquake that had struck the city and of a virulent plague that had been awakened from some hitherto unknown underground cavern, blunting the desire of anyone to look too closely at what was happening in the desert.

One of the Council's first breakthroughs was the discovery of a great repository of books left by the city's previous inhabitants. Duer's Library, named after the explorer who first unearthed its hallowed halls, was a network of vaults and towers that were practically bursting with strange knowledge. A team of scholars worked around the clock for months, clearing collapsed stacks and diligently piecing together the eldritch tongue of those who had constructed the miraculous library.

At the same time, the Council's explorers began cataloging the city and its surrounding areas. Beneath the city, they discovered an entire network of sewage chambers, conduits, passages, and catacombs. Many of these first explorers became lost in those twisting labyrinths, but those who emerged safely from the darkness brought maps that would become invaluable for future explorers.

All the while, the archmages of the Council set themselves to stabilizing the Breach. Without any magical support, the Breach had begun to shimmer and quiver erratically after every passage. There was a concern that too frequent travel might cause the Breach to collapse in on itself or, worse, to rupture even further.

After much debate and research, the Council found a solution to their problem. Months of toil went into the construction of a massive stonework plinth and archway, carved deeply with mystic runes and sigils, which they built up around either side of the rift. When the last enchanted stone was fitted into place, the Breach finally stabilized.

By then, the explorers had begun to slowly filter their way back into the city. Some of their number returned laden with riches, some returned with harrowing tales of strange creatures or former Council members who had formed a cult in the distant mountains. Others were simply never heard from again.

The greatest discoveries came from the band that wandered the farthest afield. Deep within the southern Badlands, surveyors had come across a deserted town, a few crumbling shanties and little more, perched near a mound of cracked and broken earth. In the center of the barren hillock was an abandoned hole leading deep into the earth.

The burrow was a mine shaft of sorts, and at its lowest point, the men found a cache of Soulstones, the same mythic stones that Abyssinia had discovered one hundred and forty five years earlier. These Soulstones, however, were fully intact, and as the Council members studied them, their scholars pointed out references to the stones in some of the texts they had managed to decipher.

The Council knew from the stories and myths of Abyssinia that those in the possession of Soulstones could channel incredible amounts of magic, and they were even more potent still in Malifaux. Realizing that they would need more people to properly survey and mine the magical gemstones from the ground, the Council decided to share their discovery with the rest of the world.

A New Age (1788 to 1790 AD)

The Council's announcement shocked the world.

Every tavern, saloon, town square, and boudoir was abuzz with debate. Pamphlets and newspapers were printed in abundance, either praising this new turn of events as the next step in human progress or decrying it as the utter ruination of mankind. Priests, rabbi, and khatib struggled to make sense of not only the knowledge that souls were real, as evidenced by Soulstones, but that there was an entire world beyond their own.

Diplomats, envoys, and politicians from all across Earth traveled to Malifaux to investigate the Council's claims. They were shown the wonders of Malifaux and were bewitched by demonstrations of magic the likes of which had previously been found only in fable and legend. They promised to share the secrets of magic and Soulstone with these nations, provided that they sent their citizens to Malifaux.

In short order, the abandoned city had become a thriving human settlement. First in the hundreds, then in the thousands, travelers made their way to Malifaux. The ruins of Santa Fe were built back up into a similarly thriving city whose only purpose was to support the city a stone's throw and another dimension away. The Council drew upon their potent magics to bring water up from below the desert, creating vast stretches of farmland whose only purpose was to feed the residents of Malifaux.

THE HISTORY OF MALIFAUX

The mining of Soulstones was backbreaking work, but the Council paid the workers well, and boom towns sprung up around new veins almost as fast as the surveyors could discover them. The largest of the Soulstones were kept by the Council to fuel their own power, but others were shipped to Earth by the cartload and then divvied up among those world powers who had chosen to support the settlement of Malifaux.

Everywhere, people experimented with Soulstones, grinding them up as alchemical components, medicine, or as power sources for increasingly complex machines. Across the world, people with no previous talent for magic drew upon the energy stored within the gems to become powerful and influential mages. Some of these mages even began teaching others how to manipulate the unseen magical energies around them, creating distinct schools of spellcasting, each with their own techniques.

Benjamin Hanks, a Connecticut clockmaker, was responsible for the activation of the first construct. There had always been a great deal of debris around Malifaux that resembled piles of broken or inert machinery.

When Hanks fitted one of these machines with a Soulstone and tinkered with it, however, it was discovered that the debris was, in fact, a fully functional mechanical marvel. Many of the machines discovered in this fashion were simple; tiny servitors or mechanical replicas of different animals. A few, however, were fearsome clockwork titans capable of wielding an assortment of vicious weaponry.

The construction and animation of these constructs soon became vogue in the city, and functioning machines were sent back through the Breach by the droves, as curiosities for kings and courtiers, machines of death for generals and warlords, and objects of careful study for scholars and engineers.

Gradually, the pioneers coming through the Breach began to settle further and further from the city proper, often hoping to strike it rich by discovering a Soulstone vein. As they ventured further afield, reports of fantastical creatures and mythological monstrosities began to filter back to the taverns and public houses of the city. At first, these reports were laughed off, but soon the missing settlers and frantic stories became too great in number to ignore. Begrudgingly, the Council was forced to admit that Malifaux seemed to be inhabited and that the natives were not friendly.

They borrowed a term from Earth's past to describe the natives of their new home: the Neverborn.

The First Resurrectionist (1791 AD)

As if the appearance of hostile natives was not enough, a new threat emerged from underneath the city itself in 1791. It was common knowledge that the sewers beneath Malifaux City were a labyrinth of twisting and dangerous passages, but there were rumors, fueled by the first explorers of that subterranean maze, of forbidden knowledge interred within the lowest crypts. A few power-hungry seekers of ancient secrets took it upon themselves to discover the veracity of these claims, and one man, his name lost to the ages, had the terrible misfortune to find the knowledge he sought.

Exactly what happened in the darkness of those buried vaults is known only to that necromancer, though various penny dreadful novels throughout the years have made their own dramatic speculations. Some stories claim that the ancient corpse-guardians of the vaults rose up from the slumber of death to attack him, while others have speculated that he made some deal with death itself for the power he wielded. Whatever the case, the nascent necromancer escaped the Necropolis with a single tome that contained the secrets to life after death.

The unnamed necromancer used the blasphemous spells contained within the tome to raise an army of shuffling undead corpses. This unliving horde attacked the Council fortifications en masse, and all who fell before the undead legion rose and joined their ranks. The putrescent zombies attempted to tear the city apart, brick by brick, and as their numbers swelled, it looked as if they would succeed in turning the city into a necrotic monarchy of darkness, death, and despair.

The whole city rose up in defense of their new home. Members of the Council unleashed powerful magics, and their mercenaries manned battlements and sacrificed themselves to protect their employers. Even with all the power of the Council, however, the weight of attrition was against them, and it appeared unlikely that anyone would survive the onslaught. Desperate meetings were held in the besieged Council chambers as the surviving mages debated whether they should close the Breach, sacrificing thousands in order to keep the relentless dead away from Earth.

What turned the tide were the defenders that rose up, unexpected, from the city's populace. Miners brandishing pickaxes and musketmen firing flintlock rifles fought shoulder-to-shoulder with fire-wielding wizards and clockwork automatons. Whenever things looked their direst, whenever another battle line seemed sure to be swept away by the press of undead flesh, another hero emerged, as if placed into the fray by destiny itself.

During this battle, the Nephilim known as Lilith drew upon her considerable magic to assume a human form, allowing her to walk among the defenders of Malifaux City without alarming them. She was at the forefront of multiple battles, scything down putrefied corpse-soldiers with frenzied, gleeful abandon. When the battle was won, she disappeared into the shadows and reappeared wherever the fighting was thickest. She gave no sign of understanding any of the languages spoken by her impromptu comrades during these battles, and any attempts to thank her or offer her aid were met with a disgusted sneer.

It was a hard-fought battle, but when the dust had settled, the nameless necromancer had been defeated by the combined might of the Council and the new champions of the age. Unfortunately, the dark secret of necromancy did not die with that villain, and, like the undead he shackled to his will, it would rise up years later to terrorize humanity anew.

An Age of Heroes (1792 - 1796 AD)

After the defeat of the necromancer, the city of Malifaux was rampant with danger and adventure.

It was a time of grievous villains. The dark mistress, Astarte, activated a colossal machine buried beneath the southern part of the city and nearly unleashed a terrifying, immortal weapon from the days of the Tyrant War onto an unsuspecting populace. Jean-Philip Archambault, the Quebecois madman, terrorized the streets of the city alongside his Legion de Morts Vivant, a pack of skeletal warriors, which Archambault had animated using the infamous Grimoire that he had stolen from the corpse of the first necromancer.

Evil men and women almost seemed to haunt the city, as if the necromancer's failed attempts to seize control had somehow been the catalyst that brought out the worst of humanity. The shadows of Malifaux seemed to grow darker, and soon, it wasn't safe to tread the city's cobblestone streets at night.

When things are darkest, however, even the smallest candle seems to burn brightly. The heroes that had arisen to defeat the necromancer had not abandoned the city, and colorful personalities such as the Jack o' the Axe, the stunning Lady Zorra, and Devilish McGuinne stepped forward to defend the weak. They fought for their own reasons, sometimes for truth or justice, but just as often for their own glory. Whatever their motivations, however, the people were grateful for their aid. They saved countless lives by dint of their courage and cleverness, and long after they perished, their legends continued to inspire others.

Amidst the heroes and villains, there were others whose true motivations were unknown. The mysterious Clockwork Queen seemed motivated by desires that found her on both sides of the conflict, and the puzzling exploits of the Masked Rider were inscrutable in their purpose. Perhaps most telling was the appearance of Kenshiro, the Weeping Blade, who arrived in Malifaux bearing a very special sword: the Masamune Nihonto. The blade and the swordsman were locked in a battle of wills, but Shez'uul was far stronger than Kenshiro, and each day, it eroded more of its bearer's mind and soul.

THE HISTORY OF MALIFAUX

Paradise Lost (1797 AD)

While the residents of Malifaux City were struggling with villains of their own making, a far greater battle was being waged elsewhere. Some of the Council members who had fled from the initial battles over the city had traveled north, across the rolling scrubland hills, all the way to the foothills of the great Ten Peaks mountain range. The closer they came to the mountains, the more clearly they could hear the voices on the wind calling out to them.

As a group, the archmages braved the high altitudes, treacherous mountain paths, and chilling temperatures to climb further up the peaks, following the voices. When they arrived at the summit of the tallest peak, however, they found the spectral form of the Tyrant December waiting for them. December whispered to the archmages, promising them great power if they could free him from the mountain winds which bound him.

It took the better part of two long years, but the archmages were eventually able to break the bindings that had kept December imprisoned for so long. Roaring with victory, December's spirit descended upon them, shattering the spirit of the strongest sorcerer in an instant as the Tyrant possessed his body and forced the others into submission. Those who refused to kneel to the Tyrant were butchered and devoured by his chosen proxy.

Things had changed a great deal since December's binding, and the arrival of humans had brought with it an opportunity. The creatures themselves were fragile and worthless, and though his proxy soon grew fat on their flesh, it did nothing to sate the Tyrant's ravenous hunger. The portal they had punched between dimensions, however, was a font of magical energy, and December believed that by consuming it, he could ascend to true godhood.

Swelled by December's influence, the winter of 1797 was a particularly bitter and cold one for Malifaux. Those who were able took shelter in their rime-mantled homes or taverns, their hearths raging to keep the deathly frost at bay. Those without proper shelter made attempts to warm themselves by burning trash or debris in abandoned tenements, trying, with desperate need, to stave off frostbite and an icy, benumbed death.

At the very apex of the weather's cacophonous bluster, December's proxy floated into the city, held aloft by the roaring mountain winds. The Council and the other heroes of the city were huddled in their homes, warming themselves by the fire as their doom floated unopposed past their frosted doors.

The Neverborn, however, had learned of December's escape and were prepared for his attempt at ascension. Lilith and her sister, Nekima, appeared from the shadows, attacking his proxy and his followers with a small army of monstrous Nephilim. It was a brutal battle, for though December was little more than a specter, he was still a formidable opponent.

Using strong winds to push the Nephilim away, December pounced on the stone archway that kept the Great Breach stabilized and began to feed upon its energies. Had it not been for the sudden appearance of Kenshiro and the Masamune Nihonto, December might have succeeded in his plan to ascend and rule over all of reality.

Shielded by the influence of the Tyrant within his blade, Kenshiro was able to cut through December's winds and advance on the Tyrant's proxy. Though December panicked when he sensed the presence of another Tyrant, he relaxed when he realized that Shez'uul was still trapped within its prison. December unleashed a blast of icy wind at Kenshiro, intending to tear the man apart with shards of ice, but he had underestimated the swordsman's speed and resilience.

Even as the ice shards impaled and killed Kenshiro, the swordsman raised his sword and brought it down in a killing stroke. The magical blade cut through the magical protections surrounding December's proxy, slicing the man in half and severing December's only connection with the mortal world.

December had invested much of his power into his proxy, and with the man's death, December's influence was greatly weakened. In his rage, December spent what little power he had to summon up one last gale of wind, hurling the Masamune Nihonto back through the Breach and out of his fading sight.

In the aftermath of the battle, Lilith and Nekima took stock of the situation. Humanity had invaded their home less than a decade earlier, and already they had come under the sway of multiple Tyrants. December had been freed from his chains, and their world had nearly met its end.

The two sisters came to an agreement: humanity was too dangerous to be allowed to live. As they debated how to seal off the Breach, they were approached by a human witch named Zoraida. The witch claimed that she could seal the Breach through a powerful ritual, but only if the Neverborn agreed to her terms.

THE HISTORY OF MALIFAUX

The sisters listened and agreed. With a devious smile, Zoraida gathered the necessary components for her ritual, which harnessed the aetheric energy left in December's wake and turned it back against the portal. The stone archway that kept the portal secure started to violently quake and rumble, and gradually, the rift began to shrink in size. The thaumaturgists back on Earth tried to stabilize the portal, but to no avail. Furthermore, those who attempted to cross through to Malifaux were cut off, as if the portal had been bricked over.

Meanwhile, Nekima took the rest of the Nephilim and spread out across the city, butchering every human they could find. In the morning, she hurled a corpse through the rift to send a message to the humans who had nearly destroyed her world. On its torso was carved a single, haunting word: "Ours."

The Breach lay open for a single moment longer and then closed in upon itself with an ear-rending, sonorous howl. The Great Breach was no more.

Fear and Confusion (1798 - 1802 AD)

The closing of the Breach shocked the world. One moment, Malifaux was a wellspring of magical power, and the next it was gone, an entire city of people vanishing overnight.

A great many people from all across the world had settled in Malifaux in the decade since the opening of the Breach. When the Breach closed, there was not a corner of the Earth that was unaffected by their loss. In every nation and every city there were men and women who had lost brothers or sisters, children or parents, or husbands or wives. Within days of the news, makeshift memorials had sprouted up all over the world.

Newspaper headlines were garish and sensational in their coverage of the loss of Malifaux. Wild rumors and theories propagated around the globe. Many refused to believe that the Breach had actually closed, thinking it a ruse or a trick intended to raise the price of Soulstones. Others believed that whatever had attacked the residents of Malifaux was coming to Earth. Apocalyptic signs and portents were preached loudly on street corners from Saint Petersburg to New Amsterdam, and the world was gripped in the throes of grief and panic.

In addition to the colossal loss of human life, the source of the world's Soulstones - the fountainhead of every major magical and technological advancement of the past decade - had been lost. Soulstones had already been one of the most sought-after commodities in the world, and in one fell swoop, it had also become the rarest. Institutions began to horde their meager supplies, and governments began to seize whatever Soulstones they could from private citizens.

Any Soulstone uses that were not deemed essential were immediately ended. This included, tragically, many large public works in addition to most medical applications. If a person was not well-connected, their Soulstones were stripped from them and added to the government stores. Nations began to look to their neighbors in an attempt to gauge just how many Soulstones they had managed to accumulate, and politicians and diplomats desperately tried to sign treaties to keep the peace.

THE HISTORY OF MALIFAUX

The Black Powder Wars (1803 - 1814 AD)

At first glance, it appeared as if the various treaties that were signed after the closing of the Great Breach would be enough to usher in a fragile peace. As time passed, however, paranoia began to set in. Everyone had seen the power that Soulstones could unleash, and no nation wished to be caught off guard should their neighbors launch an assault to claim their Soulstones. Diplomats became spies and troops were mustered along borders.

When the first shots rang out in the spring of 1803, it was as if the entire world had released a collectively held breath. Fueled by their own meager supply of Soulstones, the Bulgarian people attempted to revolt against the crumbling grip of their Ottoman rulers, triggering a series of cascading alliances and treaties that dragged all of Europe into a war that would later spread to engulf the rest of the world. With saber and flintlock, soldiers fought and died for their countries, musket lines holding against the spirited charges of fearless cavalry.

Unlike in previous wars, however, the great nations of Earth now had access to considerable magical power. Amongst the musket lines and cavalry charges, practitioners wielded eldritch energies and rained down fire upon enemy encampments. Animated constructs marched alongside flesh-and-blood troops, and some nations, such as Spain, employed necromantically-infused soldiers, ensuring that their battalions would keep marching even after death.

In Africa, a loose coalition of Soulstone-starved nations marched into Abyssinia from the north while opportunistic bandits and pirates began gnawing at its borders from the south. They found themselves facing a powerful empire that rose to the challenge of war and fought off Egypt, Italy, and the Ottoman Empire in numerous fierce battles.

Further west, the South American colonies of the Spanish and Dutch launched attacks on Brazil, while Mexico pushed northward, seizing the territory of Texas (and its numerous Soulstone warehouses) from Spain. Everywhere, armies fought and died by the thousands for gems that often were so small they could be set into a ring or brooch.

Despite the outbreak of war, however, not every nation was immediately pulled into the conflict. The nations of Japan, China, and Vietnam, for instance, banded together in a peaceful alliance through numerous marriages that tied their royal houses together with bonds of blood, becoming the Three Kingdoms. This kept eastern Asia peaceful for many years, but eventually, the increasing weakness of their neighbors could not be overlooked. Near the end of the war, the Three Kingdoms broke their stalemates and truces and marched on Eastern Europe, Russia, and Western North America.

To the victors went the spoils, not the least of which was a cache of freshly-powered Soulstones, for death was a constant on the battlefield. The Black Powder Wars, as they came to be called, were a time of diplomacy, spycraft, and open warfare the likes of which had a lasting impact on Earth.

The Rise of the Guild (1815 - 1896 AD)

When the dust had settled, a number of national borders had slightly changed, but the one clear victor wasn't a nation at all: the Guild of Mercantilers.

While the Black Powder Wars were started for national interests, the war was soon hijacked by a second, hidden conflict that raged around the world at the same time.

A handful of hidden cabals and secret societies had spurned the Council's call to restore the world's magic, thinking it to be either a foolish endeavor or part of some elaborate trick. When the Council succeeded, they were incensed and forced to spend the next decade scrambling for Soulstones like commoners. Other groups had formed around Council members who had fled back to Earth during the initial battle for the city.

While the Breach was still open, these shadowy organizations had wanted to seize control of Malifaux and its Soulstones, but the power and backing of the Council and its archmages had made that prospect dangerous at best and suicidal at worst. After the Breach's collapse, however, these shrouded syndicates saw their chance and redoubled their efforts at amassing power.

The most important generals and politicians of the Black Powder Wars were brought into these cabals, where they could seize control of Soulstones and use magical powers for their own purposes. It was not one conspiracy, but several, and their members used politics, swords, pistols, and lies to outmaneuver each other and the nations they pretended to serve.

By the end of the war, one of these sects had gained de facto control over the vast majority of the world's remaining Soulstones, and with it, the world itself. The Guild chose England for its central headquarters and seeded their people into the courts of every major nation on Earth. As the world began to rebuild, laws were passed that forbade Soulstone ownership by anyone without Guild authorization. Anyone caught violating this ban was executed, often in the presence of the very Soulstone they had illicitly obtained.

The only way for a nation to gain access to Soulstones was to accept Guild liaisons. At first, it was only one Guild agent who would ensure that the nation's Soulstones were only used in a prescribed manner, but as the years passed, more and more liaisons and inspectors were required, until eventually every major nation had an entire cadre of Guild operatives within its court. These agents took to dictating the policies and politics of kings and presidents, and those who refused to dance to the Guild's tune found themselves cut off from its Soulstones. Worse yet, they were frequently punished for their insolence with severe embargoes by whichever of their neighbors proved more willing to follow the Guild's guidelines.

Gradually, the Guild's iron grip tightened around the world. By dictating the movements of other nations' armies, the Guild was able to bring disobedient countries such as India and the Three Kingdoms to heel, turning them from independent nations into occupied police states. Only Abyssinia seemed able to resist their influence, and the Guild had no interest in antagonizing the advanced nation so long as they were content to limit their influence to Africa.

In under a century, the Guild had brought peace to Earth, but it was the peace of a prison, enforced only because none of the prisoners had the power to defy their jailers.

The Breach Reopens (1897 AD)

With all of the Guild's power, they were still unable to reopen the Breach. They made many attempts to force the portal back open over the following decades, both by repeating the original ritual and by devising new ones. Despite all of their power and all of their Soulstones, however, Malifaux remained closed to them, like a door that had been firmly wedged shut.

One century after its calamitous closure, just as the Guild seemed ready to abandon its efforts once and for all, the Breach suddenly and inexplicably reopened. The Guild quickly enacted the protocols they had prepared for such a possibility. Armed forces that had been deployed across the world were immediately recalled to guard the Breach, and high officials met in secret to debate the meaning of its reopening.

Despite all of their precautions and planning, a great panic swept through the Guild. Its leaders used all of their influence to send thousands of soldiers and tons of ammunition through the Breach in the expectation that the Neverborn would either be waiting for them or would soon learn of the portal's opening and launch an attack. Hundreds of thaumaturges and mages, meanwhile, worked to stabilize the integrity of the portal.

When, after a full month, there had been no sign of any sort of Neverborn army, the Guild created the Malifaux Resettlement Corps, armed them with heavy weapons, and sent them scrambling through the Breach to begin scouting the city.

The city was empty. There were a few signs of a recent battle - fresh bloodstains on stone walls, scatterings of shell casings, hastily erected barricades - but no corpses, either human or Neverborn. The city had once been home to thousands of people, but whatever had happened to them, there were no bodies to be found, save for a single corpse found hanging in a twisted tree near the portal's opening. The Resettlement Corps returned to Earth and made its report, and the Guild moved quickly to secure the city.

The Resettlement Corp swelled as the Guild sent more and more of its soldiers sweeping through the city, checking every building for Neverborn before moving on to the next. Smaller groups skirted the edges of the city and began clearing sections along the southern wall, intending to push any Neverborn northward toward the river, where they would have no cover and could be easily dispatched by the larger forces on the opposite bank.

Throughout the entire operation, however, the Guild never encountered anything more dangerous than a few rats. Once the first districts were secure, the Guild sent engineers and expendable laborers through the Breach to begin construction on a central fortress from which the Guild could manage the reclamation process. The citadel, which was christened the Guild Enclave, was soon bustling with personnel, including the newly appointed Governor-General, Herbert Kitchener.

The Industrial Zone began turning out weapons, ammunition, and steel rails for the reclamation effort, and hundreds of civilian workers were brought in to keep the assembly lines rolling at all hours of the day. These workers needed other people to make their food, tend their wounds, mend their clothes, and pour their drinks, and somewhere along the way, the city passed from a military garrison into a full colony.

Eventually, the Guild realized that there were no threats lurking in the shadows of the city and turned their attention toward the real prize of Malifaux: its Soulstones. The nations of Earth, eager to regain access to Malifaux, supplied the Guild with a workforce of convicts and indebted laborers, and scores of troops were

THE HISTORY OF MALIFAUX

redirected from the resettlement effort and marched north to serve as guards and supervisors in the newly reopened Soulstone mines.

The mines were more or less intact from the days of the first Breach, but the Guild cared far more about results than safety in those first days. The resettlement process had all but drained the Guild's coffers, and its leaders were eager to see the results of their investment. Cave-ins, asphyxiation, and flooding claimed nearly a third of the early diggers, an acceptable figure by the Guild's estimation.

A Convenient Quarantine

As more and more of the Resettlement Corps left to watch over the convict miners and their indentured peers, the soldiers remaining in the city received orders to cease their advancement and fortify their current position. It soon became clear that the Guild had no real interest in continuing the push into the uncleared areas of the city, which drew the ire of those living in the cramped and overcrowded slums that had sprung up in the Resettlement Corps' wake.

The Governor-General settled the matter by proclaiming that the unsettled areas of the city were filled with monsters and nightmares and were too dangerous for settlement. To reassure the citizenry, he commanded the Resettlement Corps to turn their temporary barriers and blockades into a permanent barricade and announced that the dangerous parts of the city would be quarantined. When the last of the barriers had been erected, the Governor-General disbanded the Corps and restructured them as a constabulary force, marking the end of the Guild's resettlement efforts and the beginning of the Guild Guard and the Quarantine Zone.

The Growing City

As time passed, the Guild slowly expanded the habitable portions of the city. A grouping of smaller corporations had come to Malifaux to make a name for themselves, and the Guild allowed them to build their homes and offices along the city's northern perimeter.

Using whatever resources they could purchase, these industrialists built up a neighborhood that, to this day, looks more like a frontier town than part of a larger city. Though many attempts were made to come up with a catchy name for the district, everyone just ended up calling it the New Construction Zone.

This area was not the only district that would come to be known as the New Construction Zone, however. To the south of the Industrial Zone was a stretch of burnt and collapsed buildings, many of which seemed to have fallen off into the nearby river. Some of the settlers saw promise in the devastation and descended upon the district with saws, hammers, and wooden planks. They cut away the collapsed buildings, and in their place, they built a haphazard collection of densely packed homes and warehouses.

The confusion between the two districts soon gave way to further clarification: the ordered settlement built along the northern walls of the city came to be known as the Northern New Construction Zone - or the "NCZ" for short - while the ramshackle maze of buildings that jutted out over the river became the Southern New Construction Zone, or the "SCZ."

In other areas, the residents of the city simply moved into whatever buildings they found waiting for them. The Guild wasted no time in laying down rails that would enable them to more safely and easily ship Soulstones from the northern mines back through the Breach, and people settled around these lines, both in the Northern Hills and within the city proper.

Special Divisions (1898 AD)

As the city grew and prospered, the old threats of Malifaux once again reared their ugly heads. Among the first were the Neverborn, which began attacking the settlers who braved the desolate Badlands and the loggers who traveled into the Knotwoods at the city's western edge. Rather than deploy their own troops to deal with the scattered reports of attacks in the middle of nowhere, the Guild instead chose to institute a generous bounty on Neverborn corpses.

There had always been people willing to travel to Malifaux in the hopes of starting a new life, but with the high price the Guild was paying to those willing to kill monsters, they suddenly had the attention of every mercenary, bounty hunter, soldier of fortune, and big game hunter across Earth. They flocked to Malifaux in an attempt to prove their mettle and earn a fortune, and in doing so, the core of what would become the Neverborn Hunters came to exist.

It was an exceedingly dangerous profession, and most of those who signed the Guild's charter and accepted their tin badges and shoddy shotguns never returned from their first hunt. The notable exception was Perdita Ortega, a small wisp of a girl who somehow managed to put three fully grown Neverborn into the ground within her first week. With the money she earned from those first kills, she purchased a quality pistol and started cutting a swathe of death through the Neverborn in the Badlands.

Much of the money that Perdita earned from her kills was sent back through the Breach to purchase passage for the rest of her family. First it was just her brothers, but then her father, her cousins, even her grandmother had made the trip into Malifaux. With each new Ortega, the family became progressively more capable and deadly, until eventually the Neverborn had learned to fear their name.

The Ortegas settled in the blasted lands of the Badlands and turned their profits toward the construction of a fortified ranch, which they named Latigo. Though technically free agents, the Guild turned Perdita and her family into heroes and reaped the benefits of their larger-than-life exploits, which proved that mankind no longer had anything to fear from Malifaux's natives.

The Neverborn were not the only enemy that reemerged in those early days of resettlement. The rotting dead were once again spotted walking the streets of the city, but unlike previously, where they served a single master, they now shuffled to the commands of an entire cabal of necromancers that operated secretly, under the veil of darkness.

The emergence of the Red Chapel Killer, a serial killer with a flair for the dramatic and a taste for prostitutes, inspired dozens of independent newspapers to decry the inability of the Guild Guard to protect them. When it was revealed that the Red Chapel Killer had not only murdered multiple prostitutes and young women but had also animated their corpses into shuffling zombies, the outcry became so deafening that it reached all the way back to Earth.

In response, the Governor-General outlawed independent newspapers and set up the Department of Public Relations, which was tasked with publishing a daily newspaper - the Malifaux Daily Record - and producing content for the city's aethervox station, ostensibly to ensure that the city's residents would have access to "impartial" news. The Department of Public Relations was also tasked with monitoring the aethervox stations for seditious broadcasts and with locating and destroying anyone attempting to slander the Guild's reputation.

It was only when the Governor-General's personal staff was killed and reanimated as mindless undead by a particularly brave necromancer that the Guild finally took notice of the threat building within their city. Dubbing the necromancers the "Resurrectionists" in a public aethervox speech, the Governor-General announced the formation of a task force designed to hunt down these rogue sorcerers: the Death Marshals.

The Governor-General placed this new "special division" under the direct leadership of Lady Justice, a mysterious swordfighter who appeared among the Guild's ranks seemingly out of nowhere. Though blind, Lady Justice seemed to possess an uncanny ability to sense things that others could not, and with her companion, the Judge, at her side, she set about recruiting

THE HISTORY OF MALIFAUX

promising candidates from the Guild Guard and the city's mercenaries.

There were countless rumors surrounding Lady Justice: some claimed that she was a former necromancer who sought to atone for her sins, while others whispered of a terrible confrontation with a Resurrectionist that had claimed the woman's family and her eyes. Still others whispered that Lady Justice was teaching the Death Marshals the same dark magics used by those they hunted and that her eyes had rotted away from overuse of those dark magics.

Whatever the truth, the Death Marshals proved to be remarkably effective against the Resurrectionists. The number of zombies walking the streets sharply fell, and despite their grim visages and stoic natures (or perhaps because of them), the Death Marshals soon became popular favorites of the people. Lady Justice's image was blazoned across banners all throughout the city, reassuring the populace that the Guild would not tolerate those who violated the dead.

Not all of the Guild's so-called Special Divisions were as well received by the populace, however. Early in the resettlement process, the Guild noticed that even people without any sort of magical training were starting to develop magical powers. There had been rumors of such things occurring in the days of the first Breach, of course, but the Council took a fairly liberal approach to magical study, and in any case, most of the people who settled in Malifaux in those days weren't the sort to start much trouble with their neighbors.

A good portion of the people who came through the second Breach, however, were convicts who had been brought to Malifaux against their will. When these men and women realized that they could turn invisible, throw fireballs, or transform their bodies into those of deadly animals, they turned against their Guild overseers and jailers.

In a matter of weeks, chaos had engulfed the Guild's mines, slowing their Soulstone production to a trickle. Countless convicts escaped into the wilds, some of them working their way back to Malifaux City or other settlements, where they posed as legitimate and respectable citizens. Others reveled in the new power they had inherited and attacked the Guild and anyone else around them.

The Guild realized that they had a crisis on their hands. Bringing in more convicts only seemed to make the matter worse, as the problem just repeated itself over again with new faces. Eventually, the Guild opened up its mines to paid workers to ensure that they remained functional while they dealt with the problem at hand.

The solution came in the form of a headstrong woman by the name of Sonnia Criid. Criid had come to Malifaux in search of arcane lore and Soulstones, and she had already launched a number of solitary excursions into the Quarantine Zone and Necropolis beneath the city in search of the relics of Old Malifaux. Each time, she returned with a tome, relic, or ritual that offered new insights into the nature of magic, as if the ancient books of the city were somehow calling to her.

The Guild placed Ms. Criid in charge of its newly formed Witch Hunter Task Force, earning her loyalty with the promise that she would be given access to every spell, tome, and artifact she recovered from the rogue spellcasters. Criid took advantage of the situation, commandeering room after room in the Guild Enclave for her ever-expanding libraries, as well as a room in the deep basements that she called the Yellow Crypt.

The Witch Hunters quickly became the least popular of the Guild's Special Divisions. Criid was ruthless in her persecution of people who used unlicensed magic, and countless families were destroyed when Criid or one of her subordinates appeared, declared someone to be a spellcaster or witch, and hauled them away without any sort of trial or defense. Many were executed, but the strongest were taken to the Yellow Crypt, a warded room in the Enclave's basement. There, Criid burned away the sorcerer's magic and mind, leaving them a charred and broken creature that she dubbed a Witchling Stalker.

The Rise of the Union (1899 AD)

While the Guild was struggling to deal with the threats of the Neverborn, the walking dead, and rogue spellcasters, another faction was growing to power in the shadows. The convicts the Guild had shipped to Malifaux to work in the Soulstone mines had proven to be too great in number for the Guild to handle, and in order to meet their production quotas, they were forced to hire greater numbers of independent miners and workers.

As the people settling in the Northern Hills banded together to support one another, so too did the workers in the mines band together for mutual safety. In the darkness of a mine there are countless things that could go wrong and take a miner's life, and often, the only way to prevent disaster was to trust that everyone else in the mine would have your back if things went wrong.

These bonds between miners, whether convicts or free workers, were cemented by the frequent accidents and tragedies of those early days. Cave-ins and other disasters drew the survivors together, and it wasn't long before entire settlements had banded together in a common purpose: to keep the miners and their families safe at all times.

This sense of comradery grew rapidly, and the Guild failed to see the danger in what was happening before it was too late. When a group of miners became trapped underground for days after a torrential rain flooded their mine, the story spread like wildfire. All across Malifaux, people heard how the Guild had forced the miners into the flooding depths, insisting that a bit of rain wasn't any reason to stop working.

One of the men that escaped the mine, Erick Ulish, rallied his fellow workers around the idea of a union that would provide all of its members with mutual support and safer working conditions. The idea caught on, and soon most of the Northern Hills had come together under the banner of the United Miners Union.

Within a few months, the Union had brought in enough money via membership dues to finally address the safety concerns of the Guild's mines. They began hiring engineers to help create more stable passages, better lighting, and a solution to the constant threat of cave flooding. It was into this environment of need that Doctor Victor Ramos appeared, bringing with him a cadre of skilled and loyal engineers.

There wasn't a man in the Miners Union who didn't recognize Ramos' genius for both engineering and organization. With much of the Union's dues going towards paying for these engineers, it only made sense to include them in the Union as well, and after a vote, the United Miners Union became the Miners and Steamfitters Union. By the time the Guild had realized what was happening, the M&SU had managed to spread its influence across nearly every mine in the north, giving it access to enough manpower and technology to make it a legitimate threat to the Guild's power.

Dr. Ramos was initially in charge of improving miner safety, and everything he touched turned to gold: he was able to leverage the threat of worker strikes into bargaining power with the Guild, which in turn lead to higher wages, increased safety regulations, and a program that would allow convicts to transition into paid laborers with good behavior. Similarly, the mining constructs that he created proved to be invaluable companions to flesh-and-blood workers.

When President Ulish suffered an unfortunate mining accident, Ramos was the natural choice for his replacement.

THE HISTORY OF MALIFAUX

Unbeknownst to either Guild or Union, Ramos was a skilled mage who was paying close attention to the Guild's newly created Witch Hunter Task Force. He felt that he and his ilk were doing nothing wrong and that the Guild's apparent vendetta against their kind was simply due to the amount of power that such mages might be able to bring to bear against them. He decided that there was safety in numbers and founded the Arcanist movement in the shadow of the growing Union. He drew its first members from miners and convicts who had manifested magical powers, shielding them from Guild attention in exchange for their loyalty and service.

Rising Tensions (1900 AD)

Gradually, Malifaux fell into an uneasy peace. The number of random people manifesting magical powers plunged dramatically, which the Guild took as a sign of the Witch Hunters' success at their assigned mission. In reality, the Arcanists were recruiting from the ranks of the miners and their families, turning anyone with useful powers into protected - and hidden - assets. Those who held the Guild in contempt had their anger channeled towards more productive ends: the sabotage of Guild property and the theft of Soulstones.

Under Ramos' leadership, the M&SU took a more political role in Malifaux and began to point out the worst of the Guild's fascist policies and tyrannical decrees. They funded rag sheets that ran smear campaigns against the Guild's leaders, staged strikes to draw attention away from Arcanist missions, and gradually tightened their grip on the Northern Hills.

The greatest achievement of the Union came in the form of the Hollow Point Pumping Station. The epic construction project was the brainchild of Dr. Ramos, who hollowed out the monadnock mountain at Hollow Marsh to serve as the structural basis for a series of gigantic water pumps. The pumps kept the caverns of the region (and thus, the nearby mines) relatively dry during the region's frequent storms and earned a great deal of prestige for both the Union and Dr. Ramos.

During the grand opening of the Pumping Station, however, an assassin's attack resulted in the deaths of dozens of Union personnel. The Governor-General and President Ramos were both present for the attack, which was fortunately blunted by the presence of a pair of highly skilled mercenaries that had been invited to the party. In the aftermath, accusations flew from both the Guild and the Union, with each blaming the other for the attack.

The murder of Duncan McSweeny, the Vice President of the Union, a few days later only seemed to ignite tensions further. All across Malifaux, the Union's workers went on strike, halting the excavation of Soulstones and turning the tension between the two organizations into outright violence.

Though the Union and the Guild would eventually reach an agreement that would see the workers returning to their mines, there were other events taking place that soon eclipsed the strike in the city's newspapers, both official and illegal.

The Red Chapel Killer, now identified as a former haberdasher by the name of Seamus, claimed the city's headlines when he murdered Molly Squidpiddge, the star reporter of the Malifaux Daily Record, during his theft of the Soulstone known as the Gorgon's Tear. More shocking still, Seamus then crashed Molly's funeral, murdered a great many of her friends, and used the Soulstone to resurrect her as a sentient undead creature.

In the years to follow, the undead reporter would prove to be a companion at Seamus' side, much to the annoyance of the Death Marshals and the horror of her surviving friends and loved ones.

Midway through the year, a convict woman by the name of Rasputina arrived in Malifaux as part of a convict shipment. Bound in chains for the crime of drowning her only child, Rasputina's sentence was deferred from incarceration to forced service in a Guild-funded saloon. After she proved difficult to tame (as the scars on her would-be patrons would attest), she was transferred to the far north, to a chain gang that worked in the shadows of the Ten Peaks.

As she toiled in the mines, Rasputina heard a disembodied voice calling to her, promising her power in exchange for service. The voice grew louder as winter approached, and eventually, she capitulated to its requests. The next morning, a blizzard blew down from the Ten Peaks, covering the mine in heavy snow and blinding the Guild's guards with icy winds. Rasputina escaped in the confusion, following the whispers of the voice up the side of the mountain.

At the summit, she found others who had been called by December, as well as the disembodied spirit of the Tyrant himself. None had been strong enough to contain his essence, but Rasputina proved to be a suitable host. She accepted December's bargain and gained considerable control over the winter winds and snow in exchange for accepting the Tyrant's essence into her soul.

THE HISTORY OF MALIFAUX

Kythera Opens (1901 AD)

After the first thaw of the year, an archaeological expedition led by Professor Heilin set out for the Bayou to investigate the ruins that had been spotted at the swamp's heart. Though not much was thought of the professor's expedition at the time, it proved to be one of the most significant events of its time.

The ruins that the professor had chosen to investigate were none other than the Kythera device. After a week of diligent study, he had succeeded in translating some of the runes carved into the towering structure. When he intoned them aloud, however, the ancient machinery of the portal ground into action, slowly reopening the dimensional portal that led to the realm of the Grave Spirit. Professor Heilin was unprepared for the structure to begin moving beneath him and fell from the top of the ruins to his death in the swirling waters below, but the rest of his expedition managed to escape to safety.

Sensing that the portal had been opened, the Neverborn, led by Lilith, tracked each member of the expedition down and murdered them with poison, in the hopes that their illness would be attributed to a toxic Bayou plant or a fearsome curse. Only one man, Philip Tombers, escaped their wrath, and then only because he was committed to the Guild's sanitarium.

Lilith was preparing to finish Tombers off when Rasputina, now flush with December's considerable powers, appeared at the head of a powerful snowstorm and attempted to claim the man for her own. The opening portal was slowly allowing the Grave Spirit to force its way into the world, and the Tyrant wished to have nothing further to do with the impossibly powerful entity that had killed its physical body.

Tombers perished in the battle, but he was resurrected into unlife as a talking head by Seamus, the Red Chapel Killer. Unbeknownst to Seamus, he was being manipulated by the Tyrant known as the Gorgon via his companion, Molly. By speaking with the animated head of Philip Tombers, Seamus was able to learn the magical phrase that would throw the gates of Kythera wide open.

Gradually, the Neverborn came to realize that the situation had progressed too far to stop: December had chosen a new host, and humanity had learned how to open Kythera. Rather than attempt to prevent the coming disaster, an almost impossible task by this point, they decided instead to manipulate fate and turn the disaster to their advantage.

One of the more powerful Neverborn leaders, the Swamp Witch, Zoraida, contacted Viktoria Chambers, the current owner of the Masamune Nihonto. When Viktoria passed through the Breach, fate reshuffled

THE HISTORY OF MALIFAUX

around her and the possessed sword she carried. Zoraida manipulated the young mercenary into an encounter with a doppleganger in the belief that the shapechanger would kill Viktoria and steal not just her form but also her sword, and with it, her destiny.

What Zoraida did not know, however, was that the Masamune Nihonto was a prison for the Tyrant Shez'uul. Rather than allow its chosen host to be slain, the sword enhanced Viktoria's strength and speed, allowing her to best her duplicate. When the blade passed through the doppleganger's body, it trapped the creature's soul instead of killing its physical form, just as it had done to Shez'uul centuries earlier. Left with Viktoria's form and memories, the duplicate surrendered to its twin, who spared its life. The doppleganger warned Viktoria about what it had been told would happen at Kythera, and together, the two of them set out for the ruins to stop the Tyrant December.

When the Viktorias arrived, they found that others had been drawn to Kythera, as well. Seamus and Molly had been captured and taken prisoner by Lady Justice and the Death Marshals, while Sonnia Criid had bested Rasputina and clasped her in manacles that prevented her from drawing upon her magic. Criid's research had revealed the true purpose of Kythera, and her conversations with Molly had confirmed her fears that Heilin's expedition had accidentally opened the portal. It was her intention to use Rasputina as her proxy in the ritual to seal the portal... a ritual that would almost assuredly cost the one intoning it their soul.

Fueled by the might of a Tyrant, however, Rasputina's power was far greater than Criid had anticipated. Once she had learned the phrases she needed to close the portal, Rasputina broke free from her confinement and called out the words that would close it. As the last of Kythera's gears ground to a halt, December felt the power that the Grave Spirit had stolen away with his death return to him, and with it, he willed himself into a physical form.

It was only the appearance of the two Viktorias and the Masamune Nihonto that saved the day. Using the blade, the two swordfighters cut December down, much as the swordsman Kenshiro had dispatched the Tyrant's host a century earlier. In the confusion, however, Molly freed Seamus from his bonds, and the Gorgon whispered the words needed to open the portal into Seamus' ear.

With a mighty shout, Seamus forced Kythera's portal wide open, heralding the entry of the Grave Spirit into the world. The personification of death itself crawled upwards from the depths of the dimensional portal. The Grave Spirit would have devoured all life in the world, were it not for Victor Ramos' sudden arrival in the Leviathan, a colossal construct that he had been building to wage war on the Guild.

Instead, Ramos turned the massive cannons of the titanic war machine on Kythera itself, shattering the device, collapsing the portal, and sealing away the Grave Spirit once and for all.

The Awakening of Tyrants (1902 AD)

The tensions between the Guild and the M&SU increased with each passing year until they finally spilled over into chaos in the spring of 1902. Union rioters took to the streets and lit fire to numerous Guild holdings, filling the Downtown district with flames. A smaller group of rioters even attempted to march on the Governor's mansion to burn it down, but they were quickly executed by Guild sharpshooters stationed on the mansion's roof.

Despite these defenses, however, the Guild still suffered a significant loss. A decorated Guild officer, Captain Gideon, turned on his employers and, in a moment of madness, murdered the Governor-General's son, Francis. Gideon was arrested for his crime, but he was brutally murdered in his cell before he could stand trial.

Amidst the riots, however, more insidious threats were beginning to awaken. With the destruction of Kythera, the Grave Spirit's influence upon the world had been lessened. For the spirits of the defeated Tyrants, it was like a heavy weight being lifted from their shoulders, and gradually, those ancient entities began to strain at the boundaries of their prisons.

Nytemare returned from its self-imposed banishment to the realm of dreams in the company of a small boy, the Dreamer, who could manipulate reality at will. Cherufe reached out from its orbital prison, touching the mind of Sonnia Criid and subtly manipulating her in ways that prepared her mind and body for her eventual possession. In a frozen lake at the center of a Soulstone geode, Witness opened her eyes and stared upwards through unyielding ice.

The shackles that had bound the Tyrants for millennia had been rattled by Kythera's destruction, and now, minds which had long ago withdrawn into the contemplation of their own misery began to look outward once more.

THE HISTORY OF MALIFAUX

The Piper's Plague

The first Tyrant to escape its confinement was Plague. The wards surrounding the Tyrant's prison beneath Malifaux City were designed to turn aside anything living that approached them, but a twist of fate bypassed them in a manner that the Tyrant's long-dead jailers hadn't intended. A burning building, lit aflame by the Union rioters, tumbled downward and smashed into the ground, shattering the street and collapsing a portion of the sewers beneath it. The ratcatcher Hamelin was in those sewers, and the resulting catastrophe knocked him into the brackish waters, which spilled out into side channels that had long ago been sealed away.

When Hamelin finally regained consciousness, he found himself in Plague's ancient, now-shattered prison. Rather than directly possessing Hamelin, Plague pushed its essence into the insects and larvae that the sewer water had carried into his prison, possessing their bodies and then forcing them to devour the rat catcher's form and essence.

Now clad in Hamelin's body, Plague was able to stroll out of his prison with minimal effort. In the weeks that followed, a terrible contagion spread out across the city. The Death Marshals initially believed the plague to be part of a new Resurrectionist plot and moved quickly to quarantine the Breach, lest the plague spread from Malifaux to Earth. The disease was more virulent than anything humanity had seen before: it was carried by rats and insects that seemed immune to its effects, but once it had infected a human host, the disease ran its course in minutes, rotting away flesh in the blink of an eye.

Soon, the plague had engulfed the entire city. Rumors spread of a man in a wide-brimmed hat who moved among the swarms of rats and infected, a pipe pressed against his lips. Soon, these glimpses of Hamelin the Plagued had given the outbreak its name: the Piper's Plague.

The Event

The Death Marshals did their best to eliminate what they believed were zombies that had been killed and reanimated by the plague. The "zombies," however, proved to be living people who had been ravaged by the disease and were now being controlled by Plague, similar to how it was controlling the swarms of rats that had boiled up out of the sewers and into the streets. The Death Marshals were horrified by the revelation, and the throngs of rats took advantage of their shock to swarm over them in waves of infected, biting fury.

In the days before Titania and the death of his mortal form, Plague had been working on an energy amplification device that would allow the Tyrant to ascend to godhood. After his death, the original inhabitants of Malifaux had turned the device to their own purposes and used it to imprison the Tyrant Cherufe.

Plague easily found half of the key to the device in the Necropolis beneath the city, and he tracked the other piece, which shaped like a small ring, to an observatory in the Forlorn district of the Quarantine Zone. The Tyrant snatched the ring from its owner, a prostitute-turned-Resurrectionist named Kirai Ankoku, and activated the device, bringing Cherufe's prison, the Red Cage, crashing down to the ground like a meteor.

Unbeknownst to Plague, however, Kirai had been touched by the influence of the Gorgon, and by drawing upon the spirits of the underworld, she was able to defeat Plague. Plague had intended to harness the amplified aetheric energy released when the cage collided with the ground and punch a hole into the aether, but in his absence, the energy exploded outward across the world in an uncontrolled purple shockwave. With no way to understand the cause of the shockwave, the people of Malifaux took to calling its appearance "The Event."

While the shockwave passed through most people without much effect, anyone with significant magical powers was "super-charged" by the wave of aetheric energy. By embracing this energy, the mages were able to temporarily shed their mortal forms and become something greater than a mere human... and something far closer to a Tyrant.

Martial Law (1903 - 1904 AD)

With Plague's defeat, the Piper's Plague decreased in potency, though it continued to spread through the city's countless rats. The slums were the worst hit, and those seeking to escape the disease unknowingly carried it from the city and into many of the surrounding boom towns. After the first infected person was discovered in Ridley, the hub town shut down its railways and barred its gates, lest the infection spread further across the Northern Hills than it already had.

While this desperate maneuver likely saved the lives of thousands of miners all across the region, it also brought the flow of Soulstones from the northern mines into the city - and thus, back to Earth - to a screeching halt. The mines continued to dig the stones from the ground, but the trains did not leave Ridley to collect the shipments. After the first two weeks, the Guild authorized

THE HISTORY OF MALIFAUX

overland transport of the growing stockpiles of Soulstone caches, but the high prices of the magical gems proved to be too much of a temptation to ignore. Entire shipments were lost to bandits, thieves, and corrupt guardsmen, as well as to the typical dangers of Malifaux's wilderness.

Even the normally distant Gremlins were shaken by the aftermath of the Event. The Red Cage had fallen upon the lands of the LeBlanc family, killing thousands of Gremlins and leaving a deep crater in its wake. Worse yet, hordes of previously unknown mechanical undead soon began to crawl forth from the underground caverns breached by the impact, forcing the LeBlancs and the nearby LaCroix into a desperate battle for survival.

The mechanical undead were not the only horrors unleashed by the Red Cage's fall, however. The Tyrant Cherufe had been imprisoned within the Red Cage, and it escaped into these subterranean tunnels, burning a path behind it as it sought out its chosen host, Sonnia Criid, the leader of the Guild's Witch Hunters. The Tyrant bound itself to Criid's soul and, drawing upon her innate talent, set out to light all of Malifaux aflame. Fortunately, Criid's second-in-command, Samael Hopkins, was able to bind Criid's powers (and thus, those of the Tyrant) behind one of the magic-dampening masks they used to capture witches.

Cherufe's possession of Sonnia was terrifying, but the Tyrant's influence had already done significant damage to the city. During the battle for the Witch Hunter's soul, Cherufe had drawn magma up from the planet's mantle, poisoning the local water table and making much of Malifaux City's drinking water non-potable.

When combined with reports of normally docile animals all across Malifaux turning feral and feasting upon the flesh of their human ranchers (the result of magical fleshwarping perpetrated by a group of Arcanist sympathizers who called themselves the Order of the Chimera) it was not difficult to understand why the Guild felt as if it was swiftly losing control of Malifaux. The streets were constantly filled with battles between the various factions of the city - the Guild crossed swords with Arcanist, Resurrectionist, and mercenary interests on a daily basis - and the strongest leaders of these groups now possessed the ability to become powerful Avatars the likes of which neither bullet nor spell seemed capable of harming.

The final straw was the Sourbreak Line Disaster. The Guild used a series of aircars - small zeppelin-like transports guided by a system of zip lines - to quickly redeploy guardsmen or ferry important people or resources across the city. On the night of the Sourbreak Line Disaster, three of the mightiest aircars all converged on the same location at once, resulting in a terrible explosion that set the night sky ablaze and incapacitated the primary aircar lines for the rest of the year.

In the wake of these disasters, the Governor-General declared Malifaux City to be under martial law. All travel in and out of the city was forbidden, save for that deemed critical to the Guild's operations (which primarily meant the importation of Guild supplies and the exportation of Soulstones). Furthermore, a mandatory curfew was put into place.

The following year brought an end to the Piper's Plague and the restoration of Guild control over the city. The restrictions on new arrivals were lessened, primarily due to the need to supplement Malifaux's severely diminished population, and gradually, new residents began to fill the streets as an uneasy peace descended on the city.

Rationing and Smuggling

The Governor-General's declaration of martial law made life difficult for those trapped in Malifaux. The Guild instituted rationing programs within the city, but the rations were notoriously small and bland. Some resourceful residents made small fortunes for themselves by boiling the water of the river and selling it back to others, and hunters and trappers charged high prices for whatever fresh meat they were able to bring back to the city.

Some of the city's residents chose to abandon the city in favor of northern settlements such as Ridley or the smaller mining towns. These settlements benefited from their rural locations, as hunting and farming were able to supplement the meager rations shipped north by the Guild.

While many people struggled to simply survive under martial law, the city's smugglers were soon thriving. The price of everyday goods in Malifaux had increased significantly, and everyone wanted something that the Guild refused to give them. Meat and alcohol were a commodity, and many smugglers turned to Malifaux's indigenous Gremlin population to provide them with fresh pork and moonshine.

The Arcanists made a great deal of money on the Soulstones they smuggled back through the Breach during this time, for the nations of Earth had begun to suspect that the same tragedy that closed the first Breach was about to strike the second and were scrambling to stockpile as many of the magical stones as possible. Faith that the Guild could keep order in Malifaux had begun to wane, and some nations - such as England - used this opportunity to declare their independence from the tyrannical organization.

The Rise of the Ten Thunders

The desperation and lack of resources caused by the Guild's policies were particularly brutal for those who lived in the slums. Sometimes, the Guild would run out of food before the ration officers reached the outlying slums, which left the residents of those districts hungry and forced to find nourishment wherever they could. Other districts - such as the Little Kingdom, which had become a haven for the city's Asian immigrants - were deliberately ignored by a handful of racist ration officers.

The people of the Little Kingdom were forced to turn to the district's street gangs for their food. These gangs gained a great deal of power in a very short period of time, and soon they had grown large enough to force those under their care to pay protection money to avoid beatings, kidnappings, and worse. Fights between rival gangs broke out every few days, and few ended without property damage or civilian casualties.

It was in this garden of chaos and violence that the Ten Thunders bloomed into existence.

Many generations earlier in Japan, the Katanaka family had been disgraced and dishonored by their use of assassins and ninja. Rather than attempt to redeem their name, they resigned themselves to the shadows and built up an extensive criminal network that spanned the breadth of the Three Kingdoms. In the course of their activities, the Katanaka discovered a stable portal into Malifaux: a hidden Breach between the two worlds that connected mainland China to the mountains north of Malifaux City.

Realizing the opportunity presented by such a portal, the daimyo of the Katanaka family had sent his daughter, Misaki Katanaka, through the dimensional rift to pave the way for her family's arrival. When word of the Guild's decree of martial law reached her, Misaki sent word back to her family to inform them that their time had come.

Moving slowly so as not to arouse suspicion, the Katanaka family began to move its people through the secret Breach, allowing them to slowly filter their way into Malifaux without the Guild's knowledge. In only a few months, they had grown large enough to begin fighting the other street gangs for territory.

The street gangs of the Little Kingdom drew upon a variety of cultures and mystical traditions to enforce their will upon the district, but the Katanaka family had access to resources far beyond anything the other gangs could match.

Calling themselves the "Ten Thunders" to disguise their true origins, the Katanaka began to aggressively expand their influence in Malifaux. The gangs who fell before them were given a single opportunity to surrender and join their organization. Those who accepted the offer - and who showed respect to their betters - were given places of influence within the crime syndicate's Malifaux branch. Those who refused had their bodies hanged in the streets as an warning to others.

Once they had secured enough land, the daimyo of the family and Oyabun of the Ten Thunders, Baojun Katanaka, joined his daughter in Malifaux to oversee the construction of the Katanaka Trading House. The structure came to serve as the syndicate's base of operations in Malifaux City, and using the trading house as cover, the Ten Thunders brought

THE HISTORY OF MALIFAUX

food and supplies through their hidden Breach and gave them freely to the people of the Little Kingdom.

As the Ten Thunders expanded their territory, more and more of the Little Kingdom fell under their control. This brought not just an end to the constant squabbling between the street gangs, but also the consolidation of a great deal of the district's vices under one roof.

The Little Kingdom had always been a haven for gamblers, prostitutes, and illicit goods, but now Ten Thunders guards stood outside the brothels and gambling dens and collected the money each night.

There were some concerns among the Guild about the aggressive expansion of the Ten Thunders, but the Little Kingdom was far enough away from the "civilized" parts of the city that they were generally ignored. The Guild Guard ceased to patrol the district, and soon they had come to an unspoken understanding with the Ten Thunders: so long as the Guild left the Little Kingdom to its own devices, the Ten Thunders would ensure that the district didn't cause any problems for the city.

Unbeknownst to the Guild, however, the Oyabun's plans were far more ambitious than the control of a single district. Baojun Katanaka wanted nothing less than to bring all of Malifaux under his control, and his daughter's reports had provided him with plenty of information on the various other factions vying for power in the city. Working subtly, he seeded his own people within their ranks and set about bribing and blackmailing anyone who seemed susceptible to such tactics.

There were missteps along the way. The most notable was the recruitment of Shenlong, a powerful fighter and Tibetan religious leader who supplied the crime syndicate with a small army's worth of monks and sohei in exchange for passage through the Breach. Unbeknownst to the Ten Thunders, though, Shenlong was simply the latest host for the Dragon, who was more than happy to use the organization as the means to return to its native Malifaux.

By the end of 1904, the Ten Thunders had become a major power in their own right, with strands of power lacing their way through the heart of every major faction and organization throughout Malifaux.

Slipping Grasp (1905 AD)

At the start of the new year, the Governor-General ended martial law in Malifaux and lifted the Guild's restrictions on travel. The announcement caused a great deal of excitement across Earth, and the Guild's Department of Public Relations announced new settlement plans that promised multiple acres of land to any settlers who were willing to work them. The price of black market Soulstones dropped dramatically, and the nations of Earth heaved a collective sigh of relief at the knowledge that the Guild had solidified its control of Malifaux.

Unfortunately, the Guild's holdings back on Earth had begun to slip from their grasp. The Guild had relied a bit too heavily upon English troops to enforce its presence in India and the Three Kingdoms, and now that King Edward VII had recalled those soldiers back to England, the Guild was forced to spread its troops thin to hold both regions. India was the first to rebel, and while the rebels were quickly crushed by the Guild's trained soldiers and pneumatic constructs, the fact that things had even gone that far was enough to place doubt into the minds of other world leaders.

Soon Russia and the Ottoman Empire had begun to distance themselves from the Guild. Suddenly the leaders of those nations were holding meetings that didn't involve Guild representatives, and their Guild-issued Soulstones began to go "missing" with alarming frequency.

Meanwhile, tensions between the Guild and the people of the Three Kingdoms continued to increase until, eventually, the oppressed peasants and workers rose up in rebellion. Led by a mysterious, masked man known only as "the Boxer," the people of the Three Kingdoms fought back against the Guild and what they perceived to be the destruction of their traditional values by "Western powers."

The Guild attempted to fight back against the revolutionaries, but the Boxer had the support of the Ten Thunders, who took advantage of the increasing danger of their homeland to recruit people with the skills and talents they needed to advance their goals in Malifaux. In essence, the Ten Thunders had gambled away the safety of their homeland in order to improve their influence in Malifaux.

Obliteration

While the Guild's troubles on Earth were occupying much of their time, another Tyrant had begun to stir in Malifaux. A woman named Tara Blake found the entrance to the prison of the Tyrant Obliteration, who had been trapped in a timeless realm crafted from its own spirit. Tara spent the equivalent of thousands of years within the realm, remaining sane as the others drawn into Obliteration's prison succumbed to madness.

Upon reaching the center of the prison, Obliteration contacted Tara and asked her to free it from its confinement. In return, the Tyrant promised to make Tara its herald in the world, giving her power undreamed of by mortals.

Tara accepted the offer and stepped forth from the prison's entrance to learn that only a few moments had passed in Malifaux. Unfortunately for her, a Guild sniper had also been lured out to the prison, and in his anger for having lost the prize he sought, he shot Tara in the heart, killing her. During her time in the prison, however, Tara had befriended a necromancer who also sought Obliteration's power, and that necromancer brought Tara back to life as a sentient, free-willed undead.

Her death was humbling, but it taught Tara the benefits of subtlety. Like December and Plague, Obliteration wished to ascend to godhood, but unlike its peers, it was willing to take a more subtle approach to its plan. Working quietly through intermediaries, Tara began recruiting others to her cause, doling out snippets of Obliteration's power in order to advance the Tyrant's hidden goals.

Crumbling Foundations (1906 AD)

During the Event of 1902, Governor-General Kitchener became an Avatar in his mansion. The manifestation was swept under the rug and all those who witnessed the transformation were executed, keeping the rest of the Guild oblivious to his new powers. With the assistance of his secretary, Lucius Mattheson, a Neverborn masquerading as a human, the Governor-General embarked on a long and arduous campaign to surpass the limits of his Avatar state and become a true Tyrant.

Kitchener's plans reached their final stage in the late winter and early spring as he traveled from one settlement to the next, awarding titles and plaques that reinforced his right to rulership through symbolic representations of power. In the town of Sunbeam, however, the Governor-General encountered severe resistance from the M&SU, which was in turn being manipulated by the Ten Thunders, who had guessed Kitchener's plans for ascension years earlier.

During the protests, the Governor-General was drawn into a battle with Mei Feng, a member of the Union and the Thunders, during which both combatants manifested their Avatars. Neither combatant was able to gain a decisive victory over the other, but the confrontation was enough to convince the Governor-General that he could no longer afford to waste time. He returned to Malifaux City and began the ritual that would transform him into a Tyrant.

Kitchener's plans, however, were undone by treachery. One of the men he had counted on to gather the various arcane relics that would lend him the power he required for the ritual was secretly a Ten Thunders agent, and that man swapped a magical relic for a few bones that had come from the physical remains of a Tyrant. When the Governor-General attempted to draw upon the relic's power, he was unprepared for the amount of power contained in the bones, and his ritual of ascension spiraled beyond his control.

Sensing the sudden burst of aetheric energy, the Tyrant Cherufe, buried in the soul of the nearby Sonnia Criid, saw its chance and attempted to ascend as well. Like two matches flaring to life next to each other, the essences of the two Tyrants melded into each other as the ritual reached its catastrophic climax.

The Burning Man

Cherufe and the newly-formed Tyrant that had once been the Governor-General fused together into something more powerful than either. The Governor's mansion exploded around the new entity as it rocketed up into space and through the dimensions, its uncontrolled power raging all around it. In a desperate attempt to cling to the last vestiges of what it had been, the entity burned its way backwards through time to when the Governor-General first began to ascend past his Avatar state: April 10th, 1906, the day of his fight with Mei Feng.

The entity, which would come to be known as the Burning Man, appeared in the skies of Earth, above San Francisco. The entity's power warped space around it, driving those susceptible to its influence (including many of the prisoners inside Alcatraz Citadel) insane. On April 18th, the full extent of the Burning Man's power was realized as a terrible earthquake struck San Francisco, devastating the city. Worse yet, the Burning Man's presence weakened the barriers between worlds, allowing monsters from Malifaux to cross over into Earth to stalk the flaming ruins of the city and feed upon the survivors.

Throughout the chaos, the Burning Man drifted above the world, its face twisted in a permanent, silent scream. Over the next few months, it appeared all over the world, sometimes drifting slowly through the sky like a herald of doom, other times simply appearing overhead

THE HISTORY OF MALIFAUX

with no warning. When it passed over New Zealand, the presence of so much magical energy awakened the slumbering Horomatangi. The slow path it burned through the skies of northern Canada forced the Native Americans below it - those whose ancestors had bred with Neverborn - to fall to the ground in agony as their Malifaux heritage violently asserted itself, awakening the shapeshifting abilities that had been buried in their blood for generations.

The worst of the damage occurred in early June, when the Burning Man's presence above London caused portals to open all around it, connecting the Earth city to the depths of the Malifaux ocean. Countless tons of seawater poured into the city, bringing with it twisted monstrosities. Many of these monsters died instantly, but some were able to adapt to surface life or slink into the ocean to spawn and multiply.

Blame and Punishment

While the nations of Earth struggled to react to the appearance of the Burning Man and the carnage and insanity left in its wake, the Guild in Malifaux found itself without a leader. The various Special Divisions immediately began to pursue their own ambitions, but the most ambitious by far was the Elite Division, which publicly accused Dr. Ramos and the M&SU of assassinating the Governor-General. Anyone with a Union membership was rounded up and placed into large holding pens in the Guild Enclave, where they awaited their day in court... and the inevitable conviction of treason and conspiracy that filled the boughs of the Hanging Tree with swaying corpses.

The Resurrectionists took advantage of this lack of leadership by launching an attack on the Guild Enclave. The undead horde gathered in the eastern part of the city and pushed westward, and everyone who fell beneath the wave of gnashing undead was promptly reanimated by the master necromancer behind the assault. The Death Marshals attempted to blunt the advance of the undead with the Guild's constructs as best they could, but it was clear that attrition was working against them.

An unexpected ally arrived in the form of the Ten Thunders, who attacked the southern flank of the undead army as the Guild lines began to collapse. The sudden assault left an opening that the Death Marshals exploited, and as the battle began to turn, the necromancer fled, leaving his zombies to the mercy of the Guild. The city had been saved from becoming an empire of the dead, much as it had a hundred years prior, but the battle had claimed many lives and left small packs of uncontrolled undead hidden within the shadows of otherwise civilized areas.

As the threat of the undead began to fade into recent memory, a prospector returned to the city with rumors of ancient Neverborn ruins that he had found deep in the Badlands. Normally, that wouldn't have elicited much surprise - Neverborn ruins were scattered all across Malifaux, and the city itself technically fell into that category - but as the prospector began to describe his find, it became clear that he had stumbled across something important.

Rumors spread quickly, and soon the city's scholars had dug out their ancient maps and translations and announced that the ruins had been mentioned in the most obscure of Neverborn texts and that they had a name: Nythera. Dozens of mercenary groups traveled into the ruins, intrigued by rumors of a great and powerful weapon that had been sealed within the ruins. The Neverborn did what they could to keep these curious humans away from Titania's prison, but two groups managed to best them through superior numbers and firepower: the Cult of December and a couple of mercenary groups, including the highly skilled Freikorps.

The Freikorps sought the powerful weapon they believed was sealed within the ruins, while Rasputina and December wished only to reinforce the magical seals imprisoning Titania. As the two groups fought, a third group of mercenaries managed to slip past them and open the ruins, freeing Titania from her millennia-long imprisonment and forcing both the Cult and the Freikorps to flee.

Though disoriented due to the many changes which had befallen her world, Titania could sense the spirits of the active Tyrants moving in its shadows. She attempted to unite the scattered Neverborn tribes beneath her banner but found resistance to the idea, for the Neverborn still remembered stories of "the bloody queen." The near-ascension of the Governor-General had spooked many of them, however, and more than a few were willing to bend their knee to the undead queen, sacrificing their freedom for the hope that Titania would save them from another apocalypse.

Midway through the year, the new Governor-General, Franco Marlow, arrived in Malifaux and began restoring order. One of his first acts was to pardon the hiding Dr. Ramos and end the trials of the M&SU, which he blamed upon "rogue elements" of the Guild. An internal investigation (and a number of executions) followed, and the Guild paid reparations to the families of those who were executed. This went a long way towards easing tensions between the organizations, primarily because the new Union president, Toni Ironsides, was surprised to find the Guild admitting fault in the situation.

THE PRESENT

On Earth (1907 AD)

The current year is 1907. The people of Malifaux live in uncertainty, for events on both sides of the Breach have shaken the foundations of both worlds.

The Burning Man drifts slowly across the sky, sowing chaos and madness in its wake. A series of cults have sprung up beneath the mysterious entity. By far the most active cult was born in the fires of London, but similar groups seem to spring up wherever the Burning Man wanders. A few even possess magic powerful enough to tap into the Burning Man's power and open portals of their own.

The sea creatures that were released into the ocean during the battle of London have begun to spread out across Earth's oceans, and reports of attacks upon fishing and military boats are on the rise. The numbers of this so-called "gibbering horde" are increasing with each passing day.

The Guild has lost control of Earth, and though they are straining to hold onto whatever power they can, the largest and most powerful nations have already started to pull away from their grasp. England and Abyssinia have already marshaled their armies and seized the lands nearest them, ostensibly in order to protect them from the monsters that have been unleashed upon them.

Rebellions have become common in India, and despite increasing restrictions and brutal massacres, the Three Kingdoms are on the verge of reclaiming their independence. Russia and the Ottoman Empire have both demanded more of the Guild's Soulstones, and in its desperation to keep the nations from following in England's footsteps, the Guild has given in to these demands. Across the ocean, American senators debate the benefits of remaining with the Guild where before such talk would have been political suicide, and the Mexican government is desperately trying to fight back against the monsters unleashed during the San Francisco earthquake.

In Malifaux

For once, things seem to be better in Malifaux than they are on Earth. The Guild has retained its control of the city, if just barely. Upon Von Schill's refusal to join the Guild Guard, Governor-General Marlow outlawed mercenaries in Malifaux, which set the stage for the Freikorps to build their own compound, Freiholt, in the Badlands.

Tensions are high amongst the Arcanists; Victor Ramos now sits in a Vienna prison after Ironsides made a backroom deal with the new Governor-General, creating a dire rift amongst the Union and the Arcanists. In response, Anasalea Kaeris has focused her rage against the Guild, burning anything and everything bearing the Ram's head symbol to ash.

The Resurrectionists have been severely hindered, as many of them were murdered by the leader of last year's attack in order to absorb their undead into his own mob. With Nicodem dead by the hands of Lady Justice, any loose ties that stitched the Faction together have been torn to shreds. Fragments of the Grave Spirit remain within Malifaux, however, continuing to whisper dark secrets into the minds of the morbidly curious, tutoring them in forbidden magics and slowly swelling their ranks once more.

Leadership has shifted within the Ten Thunders; Misaki has assumed the role of Oyabun after a decisive and deadly duel with her father. Though many have aligned themselves with the new leader, some still have to be convinced.

With Titania's ascendancy and Lilith's imprisonment, loyalties have blurred within the Neverborn. Cunning and calculating by nature, blood is quickly being spilled as roles shift and familiar masks slip. It is a grim and savage time for those clinging to the old ways.

In the Bayou, the Gremlins have become quite the nuisance, as they continue to imitate the human ways, and in what they aptly coined the "Democrazy," elected their own Gremlin-General, creating a stir in the swamp.

These shifts in alliances and leadership are but distractions to the grander schemes and growing dangers. A dark wind blows through Malifaux City, and only a narrow few recognize the violence in the air. Those monsters of yore and Tyrants of old, hiding all these years, have begun to emerge to claim what they see as rightfully theirs.

The skeins of fate have foretold this moment. The time for the Tyrants to ascend has come.

How to Play

Welcome to Malifaux, the character-driven skirmish wargame! In this game, two players fight one of the endless skirmishes for control over the towns, settlements, and places of power in the world of Malifaux.

The lure of Malifaux's valuable Soulstones has brought the powerful, the desperate, the ambitious, and the cunning to Malifaux from Earth. The Guild's control of the Breach ensures that it remains a dominant power within Malifaux City, but it is challenged on all sides by the sabotage and magical prowess of the Arcanists and the shuffling undead that serve the foul Resurrectionists.

The Outcasts, a loose collection of mercenaries and other ne'er-do-wells, sell their services to the highest bidder when not pursuing their own individual objectives, and the mysterious Ten Thunders crime syndicate works from the shadows to extend its influence throughout the city.

Not every threat to Malifaux comes from Earth, however. The ancient Neverborn will not easily surrender their lands to what they see as foreign invaders, and the Gremlins of the Bayou have become quite powerful by learning from and mimicking the humans that seized control of Malifaux City.

WHAT YOU WILL NEED

Malifaux is a skirmish miniatures wargame for two players. Players will need this rulebook to serve as a reference during their game, as well as the items listed below.

Playing Area
A standard game of Malifaux is played on a table or other playing space that can accommodate the standard 3 feet by 3 feet Malifaux table size.

Terrain
Buildings, trees, and other types of terrain are an important part of any miniatures wargame, and Malifaux is no exception. In a pinch, a stack of books or a few upside-down cups can serve as terrain, provided that each player uses a bit of imagination.

Models
You will need several Malifaux models to simulate the clash between two Crews. Each player will need their own Crew and the accompanying Stat Cards for each of their chosen models.

Tape Measure
A tape measure (preferably one for each player) marked in inches is required to determine movements, measure ranges, and so forth.

Fate Decks
Players in a game of Malifaux use decks of playing cards (called Fate Decks) to determine game results. Each player will need their own Fate Deck. Wyrd Miniatures sells Fate Decks that use the four Malifaux suits, but in a pinch, any 54-card deck of poker cards with a discernible red and black joker will suffice.

> ### What is Waldo's Walkthrough?
> Waldo here. I'm gonna help you understand all this rules-talk without having to get out a dictionary, a thesaurus, or a Kelley Blue Book to reference. Look for these boxes for the general gist of rules, not so much a thorough explanation.
>
> For more specific (and some might argue "accurate" – whatever the heck that means) descriptions on how things work, use what's written elsewhere in the rulebook, but if you're looking for a layman's view, then I'm your imp. You'll find my sections throughout these pages (just look for my gorgeous face), so give 'em a read if you find yourself scratching your head.

HOW TO PLAY

WHAT MAKES MALIFAUX SPECIAL?

Malifaux is a unique wargame for a variety of reasons that make it stand out against the other wargames that are available. Below are some of the things that make Malifaux special.

The Fate Deck

Perhaps the most defining feature of Malifaux is the Fate Deck. The Fate Deck is a deck of cards that is used to resolve the many different conflicts in the game. It is a standard poker deck, but it uses custom Suits.

The Fate Deck gives players unprecedented control over the outcomes of their actions. You can find out all about it on page 43.

The Characters

Malifaux is a character-driven wargame. The flavor and backstory of the characters stand out, giving each battle a narrative feel.

Every model in Malifaux uses a Stat Card, which is a card unique to that model that explains the character's passive and active effects. You can find a breakdown of a Stat Card on page 41.

The Encounter

Every game of Malifaux is called an Encounter, which is the scenario of the game. In Malifaux, fighting and killing are often just a means to an end. Encounters represent the objectives of every model coming to the table.

Malifaux Encounters are incredibly varied and are determined before players decide what models they are using, making each game unique. You can find out how to set up an Encounter on page 76.

The Crew

The models that each player brings to the game are referred to as their "Crew," which might represent a gang of bandits, a pack of fearsome monsters, or an organized Guild strike team.

One model in a player's Crew will be its Leader. This is usually a Master, one of Malifaux's most powerful characters. In the absence of such an inspirational figure, a Henchman is more than capable of stepping forward to lead a Crew to victory.

Soulstones

Unused points that a player does not spend to hire their Crew are converted into Soulstones, a resource that players and certain models can spend during the game in order gain various in-game benefits.

> Think of these as shiny little baubles that you spend during (and before) the game. In a standard size game, you start with 50 Soulstones and first spend them on adding characters to your Crew. Then, once you're done with that, you'll be able to do all sorts of stuff during the game with your leftover shiny baubles. You can dig into the nitty gritty of what Soulstones can do during a game on page 63.

BREAKING THE RULES

Models in Malifaux have many unique rules that override the core rules. When a special rule explicitly contradicts the core rules, follow the special rule rather than the core rule.

For instance, an Action that states it does not require Line of Sight is allowed to disobey the normal Line of Sight rules, and it may therefore choose a target in range even if it cannot see it.

If two special rules directly contradict each other, rules that prevent something from happening take precedent over rules that allow something to happen.

COMPONENTS

Here is a closer look at the various components that are needed to play Malifaux.

In addition to the components listed below, you will also need a table, some terrain, and a measuring tape. You can find more information about these materials on page 38.

MODELS

As Malifaux is a miniatures skirmish game, one of its key elements is the miniatures. Most of the game's rules describe how these miniatures interact with one another and the table. In Malifaux, a model is a collection of things, including the physical figure itself, the base it is mounted on, and that model's associated Stat Card.

Models represent the various characters that are engaging in a conflict. Each model is defined by a collection of statistics (more often referred to as stats) that represent how well its character moves, attacks, and defends.

Each model also has Abilities, which grant the character unique ways to deal with situations. This can include immunities, special ways to defend or move, or anything that isn't already described by the model's statistics.

Each model also has a number of Actions. These Actions are split between Attack Actions and Tactical Actions, which cover the active things that character can do, such as shooting a gun, clawing an enemy, or leaping through the air.

STAT CARDS

Every model has an associated Stat Card that lists the information required to use that model in the game. You can find an example Stat Card on the next page.

1. **Name & Title:** This is the name and title of the model. Some mechanics may reference the model's name.
2. **Cost:** This shows the model's Cost, which is primarily used when hiring a Crew for an Encounter.
3. **Faction:** This shows the Faction(s) to which the model belongs.
4. **Characteristics & Keywords:** Both Characteristics and Keywords are referenced by the game rules and the Actions and Abilities of models. Characteristics are presented in italics, while Keywords are presented in capital letters. Keywords are also used when hiring a Crew.
5. **Stats:** A model possesses the following stats, which represent its physical and mental strengths.

   - *Defense (Df):* This represents the model's skill at protecting itself from physical harm.
   - *Willpower (Wp):* This represents the model's strength of will and self-control.
   - *Movement (Mv):* This represents the distance (in inches) that a model may travel when taking either a **Walk** or **Charge** Action.
   - *Size (Sz):* This represents how much space it takes up on the table and is most often used when determining Line of Sight.

   Models also have stats associated with some of their Actions, which are described on page 58.

   A model's stat may never be lowered below 0.

6. **Health:** This indicates a model's maximum Health, which also tracks its current Health before it is killed.
7. **Abilities:** Models have Abilities that change how they interact with the rules, such as making the model difficult to damage or changing how it moves. A model's Abilities are always considered to be active during an Encounter unless otherwise indicated in their description.
8. **Actions:** Actions are special Attacks or maneuvers that a model can take when it Activates. Most Actions are described on the model's stat card, but there are some general Actions available to all models as described on page 58.
9. **Base Size:** This is the model's base size.

COMPONENTS

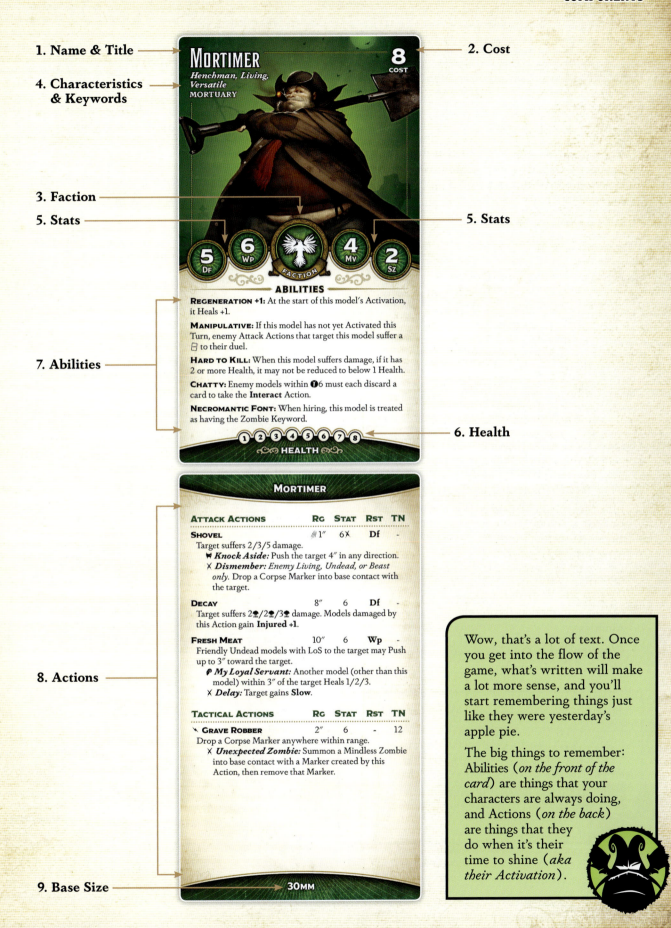

1. **Name & Title**
2. **Cost**
3. **Faction**
4. **Characteristics & Keywords**
5. **Stats**
6. **Health**
7. **Abilities**
8. **Actions**
9. **Base Size**

Mortimer

Henchman, Living, Versatile
MORTUARY

8 COST

- 5 Df
- 6 Wp
- 4 Mv
- 2 Sz

ABILITIES

Regeneration +1: At the start of this model's Activation, it Heals +1.

Manipulative: If this model has not yet Activated this Turn, enemy Attack Actions that target this model suffer a ⊟ to their duel.

Hard to Kill: When this model suffers damage, if it has 2 or more Health, it may not be reduced to below 1 Health.

Chatty: Enemy models within ◎6 must each discard a card to take the **Interact** Action.

Necromantic Font: When hiring, this model is treated as having the Zombie Keyword.

HEALTH: 1 2 3 4 5 6 7 8

Mortimer

Attack Actions	Rg	Stat	Rst	TN
Shovel	⚔1"	6✗	Df	-

Target suffers 2/3/5 damage.
- ♥ **Knock Aside:** Push the target 4" in any direction.
- ✗ **Dismember:** Enemy Living, Undead, or Beast only. Drop a Corpse Marker into base contact with the target.

Decay	8"	6	Df	-

Target suffers 2♣/2♣/3♣ damage. Models damaged by this Action gain **Injured +1**.

Fresh Meat	10"	6	Wp	-

Friendly Undead models with LoS to the target may Push up to 3" toward the target.
- ♦ **My Loyal Servant:** Another model (other than this model) within 3" of the target Heals 1/2/3.
- ✗ **Delay:** Target gains **Slow**.

Tactical Actions	Rg	Stat	Rst	TN
⬥ **Grave Robber**	2"	6	-	12

Drop a Corpse Marker anywhere within range.
- ✗ **Unexpected Zombie:** Summon a Mindless Zombie into base contact with a Marker created by this Action, then remove that Marker.

30MM

> Wow, that's a lot of text. Once you get into the flow of the game, what's written will make a lot more sense, and you'll start remembering things just like they were yesterday's apple pie.
>
> The big things to remember: Abilities (*on the front of the card*) are things that your characters are always doing, and Actions (*on the back*) are things that they do when it's their time to shine (*aka their Activation*).

UPGRADE CARDS

Upgrade Cards represent special options for your Crew. This could be specialized spells prepared just for the battle, unique or rare equipment, or special tactics.

When a model gains an Upgrade, that Upgrade is Attached to the model's stat card. This happens most often when hiring Crews, but it can also occur during the game via special Actions or Abilities. All of an Upgrade's Limitations must be followed when Attaching it, regardless of when it is Attached.

Upgrades are, by default, unique. Unless an Upgrade has the "Plentiful" Limitation, a Crew can only possess a single copy of that Upgrade.

While a model can only Attach a single Upgrade during hiring, it might acquire additional Upgrades during gameplay. No matter what, however, a model cannot Attach two or more copies of the same Upgrade; if it attempts to do so, the second copy is discarded without effect.

During hiring, a Crew can only purchase Upgrades that match its declared Faction.

Upgrade Limitations

Below is a list of Upgrade Limitations.

- **Restricted (Name):** This Upgrade can only be Attached to a model with the indicated name or Keyword. If more than one restriction is listed, the model must meet all of the restrictions in order to Attach the Upgrade.
- **Special (Name):** Special Upgrades cannot be Hired at the start of the game. They are typically Attached to models during the game by Actions or Abilities.
- **Plentiful (X):** Your Crew can possess up to X copies of this Upgrade.

> That word certainly sounds nice, huh? *Upgrade.* Like we're getting a makeover or a nice new tie. Sometimes, though, Upgrades aren't always a good thing, so keep an eye on that when you're playing. Some Crews like to put Upgrades on their opponent's models to hinder them. More like Downgrades, am I right?

Parts of an Upgrade Card

1. **Name:** This is the name of the Upgrade.
2. **Cost:** As with models, each Upgrade has a Cost.
3. **Effects:** This section explains how the Upgrade modifies the model to which it is Attached.
4. **Limitations:** Most Upgrades have one or more Limitations. This limits which models can Attach the Upgrade.

1. Name
2. Cost
3. Effects

VITALITY POTION | 0

This model gains the following Ability:
REGENERATION +1: At the start of this model's Activation, it Heals +1.

LIMITATIONS
Special (Trinket)

4. Limitations

COMPONENTS

FATE CARDS

Malifaux uses cards, called Fate Cards, to generate random numbers. There are typically four places Fate Cards might be located during gameplay: the Fate Deck, the Control Hand, the Conflict, or the Discard Pile.

Each player has their own Fate Deck. A Fate Deck is made up of 54 Fate Cards and is similar to a standard poker deck with four suits of thirteen cards each and two Jokers.

Reading the Cards

Each card has two pieces of information:

- **Value:** The number on the card.
- **Suit:** The suit on the card.

Cards of value 5 or less are called Weak cards. Cards of value 6-10 are called Moderate cards, and cards of value 11 or higher are called Severe cards.

Malifaux uses its own suits, but they translate to the standard playing card suits as below.

- *Rams (Hearts)* – 13 cards, 1 through 13
- *Masks (Diamonds)* – 13 cards, 1 through 13
- *Crows (Spades)* – 13 cards, 1 through 13
- *Tomes (Clubs)* – 13 cards, 1 through 13
- *Jokers* – 2 cards, Black Joker and Red Joker

The Red Joker has a value of 14 and has one suit of its owner's choosing. The Black Joker has a value of 0 and has no suits.

> You'll need to know Weak, Moderate, and Severe later when it's time to deal damage, but don't sweat it for now. We'll go over damage stuff on page 60.
>
> Also, think about the Red Joker as the "Oh, snap!" card, and the Black Joker as the "Oh, crap..." card. At least that's what I yell out when I flip 'em.

The Fate Deck

Fate Decks are placed face down so that none of their cards can be seen. Players are not allowed to look through either Fate Deck.

If, at any time, a player's Fate Deck runs out of cards, they shuffle their Discard Pile and place it face down to form a fresh Fate Deck. Players must offer their Deck to their opponent to cut whenever it is shuffled.

Value & Suit — EIGHT OF RAMS, MODERATE

Removed From the Game

Some game effects may cause a player to remove a Fate Card from the game. When doing so, the Fate Card is set aside face up. Cards removed from the game are never shuffled back into their owner's Fate Deck and are ignored from all game effects that do not specifically mention them.

The Control Hand

Any time a player draws cards, they are placed into that player's Control Hand (or just their "hand" for short). Similarly, if a model ever draws cards, those cards are drawn from its controller's Fate Deck and placed in its controller's hand.

A player's maximum hand size is six. If, after resolving any Action, Trigger, or Ability, any player's hand size exceeds their maximum hand size, they must discard down to meet their maximum hand size. A player may look at their hand at any time, but the contents are kept secret from their opponent.

> Do models have cards? Does the player have cards? This can get a little funky, but essentially, both are true. The player has a Control Hand. If a player has a model in their crew and that model does something like perform an Action that has them draw a card, that card is put into the player's Control Hand. This goes for discarding a card due to a game effect, too. This can be a little strange at first, but it'll make more sense as you start playing.

CORE RULEBOOK • MALIFAUX THIRD EDITION 43

COMPONENTS

The Conflict
Cards that are currently in use are considered to be in the Conflict, a clear area somewhere on the table. All information on cards in the Conflict is public knowledge.

If multiple cards are added to the Conflict as the result of Fate Modifiers, only one card is placed into the Conflict; the others are discarded.

Once the effect that caused a card to be flipped is resolved, the card is discarded.

The Discard Pile
Each player has a Discard Pile located adjacent to their Fate Deck. The Discard Pile is face up. It may not be reordered at any time during the game.

Players may look through their own Discard Piles but may not slow the game by doing so.

Whenever a card is discarded, it is placed on top of the owner's Discard Pile. If multiple cards are placed into a Discard Pile at once, they are revealed to all players before being placed in the Discard Pile in any order the discarding player chooses.

Cards discarded after Flipping, Cheating Fate, or from the Conflict are not considered discarded by the player or any specific model for the purposes of game effects.

Game effects that occur after a model discards a card only occur if a game effect specifies for a player or model to discard a card.

THE "X" VARIABLE

Some effects within Malifaux refer to X, a variable within the game that changes depending on the situation in which it is used.

If an effect ever refers to X, it will be determined by the effect itself within its text (such as defining the TN of a duel or the value of a Condition.)

X is always consistent throughout any single effect and once defined cannot change. After resolving an effect with X, the X variable reverts back to undefined until another effect defines it again.

USING THE CARDS

In the course of the game, players will use their Fate Cards in a variety of ways. Below are the most common terms associated with these cards.

Revealing Cards
When a Fate Card is revealed, it is shown to both players. If the reveal effect does not specify where the card is placed after it is revealed (such as Conflict, Discard Pile, or Control Hand), it is placed back where it originated from before the reveal effect. If multiple cards are revealed from a player's Fate Deck simultaneously, they are placed back on top of that Fate Deck in a manner so that their order does not change.

If an effect allows a player to "look at" a card, it is treated as revealing the card. However, the card is only shown to the player "looking at" it.

Flips
Flips are used to generate random results.

When a flip is required, a player reveals the top card of their Fate Deck and adds it to the Conflict to generate a random number and/or suit.

If multiple cards are added to the Conflict as the result of Fate Modifiers, only one card is placed into the Conflict; the others are discarded.

Sometimes, an effect will instruct a player to "reflip" one or more cards. When this occurs, the player discards the originally flipped card(s) and flips a new card from their Fate Deck.

Variable Profiles
Some game effects use variable profiles (such as 1/2/3) to determine their result. Variable profiles are always divided into three segments: Weak/Moderate/Severe, and which segment is used is determined by the result of a card flip.

The value of the flipped card determines which of the variable profiles is used:

- **0 to 5:** Weak
- **6 to 10:** Moderate
- **11 to 14:** Severe

Some game effects may cause a variable flip based on a value other than a card flip, effects such as these will clarify what card is used to determine the value of the variable flip.

COMPONENTS

Fate Modifiers (⊕ or ⊖)

Fate Modifiers are used to adjust a model's luck, whether beneficial or harmful based on the model's given circumstances.

There are two types of Fate Modifiers: positive modifiers (⊕) and negative modifiers (⊖). Each of these icons cancels one of the other icons, so a flip can only be affected by one or the other (or neither), never both.

For each Fate Modifier on a flip, one additional card is revealed (so a ⊕ flip would reveal two cards, as would a ⊖ flip). When multiple cards are revealed as a result of Fate Modifiers, only one card is placed into the Conflict and the others are discarded.

The card that may be used for the flip is determined by the type of Modifier. If a ⊕ Modifier was used, the player may choose any one of the revealed cards. If a ⊖ Modifier was used, the player has to choose the lowest value revealed card (if it is a tie, the flipping player chooses one of the tied cards).

The Jokers are the only exception to which cards are used. If the Red Joker is revealed, it may be chosen even if the flip had one or more ⊖. If the Black Joker is revealed, it *must* be chosen, even if the flip had one or more ⊕. If both Jokers are revealed, the Black Joker takes precedence and must be chosen.

You may never reveal more than four cards as the result of Fate Modifiers. Any additional cards that would result from Fate Modifiers are not flipped.

For example, a player with a ⊕⊕ might reveal a 4, 7, and 10. The player may choose any of these cards to use, and will probably choose the 10 for the flip. If the flip had instead had ⊖⊖, the player would have to choose the 4 as the lowest card.

Cheating Fate

Sometimes, a flip does not end up quite the way that you'd like. Malifaux gives players the chance to change their destiny by using Fate Cards from their hand to Cheat Fate.

After flipping a card, a player has the opportunity to Cheat Fate by replacing the card they flipped into the Conflict with a card from their hand.

To do this, they choose the card in their hand that they wish to Cheat Fate with and place it into the Conflict, discarding their previous card. Cheating Fate does not count as flipping a card, and it cannot be done if the flip involved one or more ⊖.

The Jokers affect the ways in which a player can Cheat Fate. A player cannot Cheat Fate if they flipped the Black Joker. Additionally, if a player flipped the Red Joker on an opposed duel (pg. 46), their opponent cannot Cheat Fate on their own flip.

Once a player has Cheated Fate or the opportunity to Cheat Fate has been declined, the player no longer has the opportunity to Cheat Fate for that flip. More information about Cheating Fate, such as who Cheats Fate first, can be found in the Duels section on page 46.

JOKERS

The two Jokers work differently than many other cards. Their rules are summarized below.

Black Joker: The Black Joker has a value of 0 and no suit. It counts as a Weak card.

Regardless of any Fate Modifiers, if the Black Joker is revealed, the player must choose it, even if there are one or more cards revealed because of ⊕ Fate Modifiers.

If the Black Joker is flipped, the player cannot Cheat Fate. If it comes up in a variable flip that involves numbers (such as damage or healing flips), the Black Joker does 0 (which cannot be modified) and does not generate any ☠ (if applicable).

Red Joker: The Red Joker has a value of 14 and one suit of its owner's choice. It counts as a Severe card.

As long as the Black Joker is not also revealed, the Red Joker may always be chosen during a flip, even if there are one or more cards revealed because of ⊖ Fate Modifiers.

If the Red Joker is flipped in an opposed duel, the opposing model may not Cheat Fate. If it comes up in a variable flip that involves numbers (such as damage or healing flips), the Red Joker does Severe +1.

"THIS MODEL"

"This model" always refers to the model which generated the game effect in which the text was written.

COMPONENTS

DUELS

Malifaux uses duels to resolve most conflicts. In a duel, a model pits its relevant stat against another number. All duels involve flipping cards and adding a stat to calculate a duel total.

If a duel doesn't have a Resist stat, it is a simple duel.

If a duel has a Resist stat, then it is an opposed duel. Opposed duels involve two different models each making a duel and then comparing their final duel totals to determine a victor.

If two friendly models are in an opposed duel, the resisting model may choose to relent before any cards are flipped. If it does, the relenting model (but not the acting model) skips Steps "A" through "D" below. The relenting model's final duel total is treated as being the same as the acting model's final duel total.

Any time a model takes a duel using a specific stat (such as **Wp**), it is said to be a duel of that type (i.e. a **Wp** duel). Similarly, if an Action has a ⚔ or 🔫 in its range, the duel is said to be a duel of that type as well (i.e., a ⚔ duel or 🔫 duel).

To perform a duel, follow these steps:

A. Modify The Duel
B. Flip Fate Card
C. Cheat Fate
D. Determine Duel Total
E. Declare Triggers
F. Determine Outcome

> In the case of duels in Malifaux, think of simple duels as the stuff you do to yourself (and your friendly models) and stuff that happens to you, and opposed duels are what's used when you're trying to mess with your opponent and their models or vice versa.
>
> There are exceptions to this (ahem, relenting), but it's not a bad way to start out when thinking about it.

Step A: Modify The Duel

Before any cards are flipped, a model that can use Soulstones may spend a single Soulstone to receive a ➕ to its flip or add a suit of its choice to its final duel total. If both models can use Soulstones, the attacking model declares whether they will use a Soulstone first.

If either player has any effects that resolve before performing a duel, they resolve now.

Step B: Flip Fate Card

Any models involved in the duel perform a flip. This flip may be affected by Fate Modifiers, as described below.

If either player was affected by one or more ➕ or ➖ Fate Modifiers, those apply now. Any player with a ➕ Modifier may choose which card they wish to use (the Active player chooses first).

Any player with a ➖ Modifier must choose the lowest value card to use. Players add their stat, the value of the flipped card, and any suits to determine their current duel total. Players must inform their opponent of their current duel total.

> Who is this "Active player" and what have they done with my son? As it turns out, the Active player is just a reference to the player whose model is currently the one Activating. You can find out more info about it on page 57.

Step C: Cheat Fate

Players now have the opportunity to Cheat Fate, as described on page 45.

In an opposed duel, the player with the lowest duel total has the first opportunity to Cheat Fate; in the event of a tie, the Defender Cheats first. Once that player Cheats Fate or decides not to, their opponent has the opportunity to Cheat Fate.

Players only have one opportunity to Cheat Fate per duel.

Step D: Determine Final Duel Total

Players then add their stat, the value and suit of the card in the Conflict, and any additional suits or modifiers together to determine their final duel total. Players must inform their opponent of their final duel total.

Step E: Declare Triggers

Any models involved in the duel may declare one Trigger for which it meets the requirements. Triggers always require one or more suits in the model's final duel total in order to work (more information about Triggers can be found on pg. 48).

If both players have a Trigger to declare, the Attacking player must declare their Trigger first.

Step F: Determine Outcome

Players must recalculate their final duel total based on any Triggers that have been declared.

The model that initiated the duel must equal or exceed the target's final duel total (in opposed duels) and the Target Number (TN) of the duel, if applicable, to succeed in the duel. If a duel's TN includes one or more suits, the initiating model's final duel total must include the suit(s) to be considered successful.

In an opposed duel, the resisting model must exceed the initiating model's final duel total to succeed.

If a model is not successful in the duel, it is considered to have failed the duel.

> ### CORNELIUS BASSE VS. PANDORA
>
> **In this example**, Basse is taking his Chesterfield Shotgun Action, targeting Pandora. Due to Pandora's Terrifying Ability, Basse must first pass a TN 13 **Wp** Duel or the Action fails. As this duel has only a TN, it is a simple duel and only requires Basse to flip cards and make decisions.
>
> Basse, fearing that he may fail the **Wp** duel, chooses to discard a Soulstone to give himself a ⏶ modifier to his **Wp** duel.
>
> Basse then reveals the top two cards of his Fate Deck (a 6 ✕ and a 9 ♛) and places them into the Conflict (the second is due to his ⏶ modifier.) Basse is able to choose either card revealed for the duel, so he chooses the 9 ♛ and discards the 6 ✕.
>
> As this is a **Wp** duel, Basse then adds his **Wp** Stat (5) to the value of his chosen card (9 ♛) to determine his current duel total of 14 ♛.
>
> The TN of the **Wp** duel is 13, so Basse doesn't need to Cheat Fate and calculates his final duel total to be 14 ♛. As the TN of the duel is 13, Basse succeeds at the duel, so he can now Attack Pandora as part of an opposed duel.
>
> Basse's Chesterfield Shotgun Action has a Stat of 6 and is resisted by **Df**. Because it is an opposed duel, both Pandora and Basse will flip cards and make decisions.
>
> Neither model chooses to use Soulstones, so they each flip a single card. Basse flips a 4 ♥ and Pandora flips a 10 ✕. Basse and Pandora both calculate their current duel totals, adding their Stat and the value of the flipped card; Basse (10 ♥) and Pandora, with a **Df** of 5, has a total of 15 ✕.
>
> Comparing their values, Basse (as the player with the current lowest duel total) chooses to Cheat Fate by placing a 10 ▦ from his Control Hand into the Conflict, discarding his previous 4 ♥.
>
> Pandora declines to Cheat Fate.
>
> Now they need to compare their current duel totals: Basse with 16 ▦ compared to Pandora's 15 ✕. Each player may then choose to declare a single Trigger. Basse may declare a ▦ Trigger on his Action, while Pandora may declare a ✕ Trigger.
>
> Neither model chooses to declare a Trigger (as neither have Triggers matching their suit), so the final duel totals are calculated (16 ▦ vs 15 ✕). Basse succeeds and is the winner of the duel.

COMPONENTS

TRIGGERS

A Trigger is an additional outcome of a duel. In order to use a Trigger, a model must have one or more specific suits in its final duel total (as noted before the Trigger's name). Only one Trigger may be declared per duel per model. There are two types of Triggers: Action Triggers and Resistance Triggers.

Action Triggers

Action Triggers are tied to specific Actions and can only be used with that Action. They are found below an Action's effect and are subject to all game effects that affect the Action (such as Incorporeal or 🗡 flips to damage). An example of an Action Trigger is listed below:

> 📖 *Surge:* Draw a card.

Resistance Triggers

Resistance Triggers are Abilities (listed on the front of a model's Stat Card) and may be used when the model is involved in an opposed duel that uses the stat referenced by the Resistance Trigger. Resistance Triggers cannot be declared by a model if they are targeted by an Action generated from their own **Disengage** Action. An example of a Resistance Trigger is listed below:

> **Df/Wp** (🐀) *Squeal: Enemy only.* After resolving, this model may move up to 3″.

Costs

In addition to the suit needed to declare them, some Triggers have an additional cost that is listed in italics after their name. These costs must be paid when the Trigger is declared or no other portion of the Trigger may be resolved. If a Trigger's cost requires the performing model to suffer damage, that cost cannot be paid if doing so would reduce its Health to 0 or below.

Special Restrictions

In addition to costs, special restrictions are also written in italics and restrict the Trigger in some way, such as limiting the Trigger so that it may only be declared if the target is an enemy model.

See page 59 for more information on Special Restrictions.

Trigger Timing

All Triggers have a timing structure written in the Trigger itself, detailed below:

- *Immediately:* These Triggers resolve in the Declare Triggers step. They often modify the duel itself in some way.

- *When resolving:* These Triggers resolve with the Action's effects (Step 5 of Action timing). These Triggers, depending on effect, may modify the effects of the Action as listed or add a new effect, so they only occur if the Action was successful. Any new effects are resolved last, unless the Trigger specifies otherwise.

- *After killing:* These Triggers happen after killing the target of the Action, as part of resolving damage timing (pg. 70).

- *After resolving:* These Triggers happen after the Action is complete, regardless of success or failure, but only if the model that declared the Trigger is still in play. If the Trigger has a target and that target is no longer in play, the Trigger has no effect.

- *After succeeding:* These Triggers happen after the Action is complete, but only if the model declaring the Trigger was successful in the duel and is still in play. If the Trigger has a target and that target is no longer in play, the Trigger has no effect.

If a Trigger does not list a timing, it is treated as an *After succeeding* Trigger.

ACTIONS GENERATED BY TRIGGERS

If a Trigger generates an Action, that Action is an independent Action from the Action that generated it. The Trigger takes effect per its timing structure, but the model taking the Action cannot do so until all other effects (including other Triggers) have been resolved.

Actions generated by Triggers cannot declare Triggers, and like all other generated Actions, they do not count against a model's Action limit.

Bonus Actions (➹) generated by Triggers may be taken even if the model has already taken a Bonus Action during the current Activation.

THE TABLE

Malifaux is played on a surface that measures 3 feet wide by 3 feet across. This space is referred to as the "table." This area is where the battle will take place.

During a game, players will need to measure, move, interact with terrain, and draw Line of Sight (LoS). The rules governing these mechanics are explained on the following pages.

MEASURING

All distances used in Malifaux are in inches or fractions thereof. Players are allowed to measure distances at any time, provided that doing so does not unduly slow down gameplay.

Measurement is almost always done horizontally from the closest point on the base of the object in question. If a player is measuring to an object, they measure to the closest point on the base of the target. If there is a vertical element, that distance is added to the distance, minus the lower object's Size or Height (to a minimum of 0).

Many times, a player will need to determine if an object is in range of another. This is referring to the distance between the two objects. An object is within range if any portion of that object's base is at that distance or closer. Any effect that references an object being "within" a distance is talking about range.

While not used often, if an object must be *completely* within a distance, all portions of that object's base must be at that distance or closer.

Two objects are said to be in base contact with each other if their bases are physically touching (edge to edge or overlapping).

A model is never considered to be in base contact with itself.

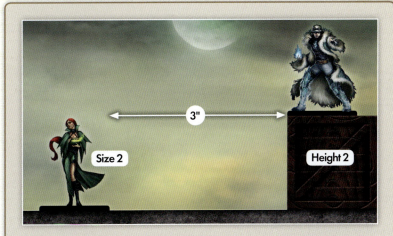

When measuring the distance between Pandora (left) and Rasputina (right), measure the distance between the two bases horizontally (3").

Because there is also a vertical difference (Height 2), that vertical distance gets added to the distance between them, minus Pandora's Size (2) since she is lower of the two models. In this case, Pandora and Rasputina are exactly 3" apart, and are therefore within 3" of each other.

In this example, Pandora and Rasputina are in base contact with one another because their bases are physically touching.

Because they are in base to base contact with each other, they are within 0" of one another.

In this example, Pandora is on a rock that is Height 1. When measuring range to Rasputina, she measures 0" of horizontal distance and adds Height 1 to her vertical distance, then she subtracts Rasputina's Size of 2, taking her down to the minimum of 0".

Pandora and Rasputina are within 0" of each other, even though they are not in base contact.

THE TABLE

MOVING

During a game, objects (most often models, but sometimes Markers or terrain) will move around the table (but never off it). Any time something changes location or is affected by a movement effect, it is considered to have moved (even if it moved 0″).

To move, measure the distance from the point on an object's base closest to the direction it will move. Move the object that distance in a straight line, ensuring that no part moves further than that distance. Models may not move through other models.

All movement is in a straight line, but unless otherwise specified, the total distance an object is moving may be broken up into multiple smaller segments, as shown in the example to the right.

It is possible for a model in base contact with another model to move around that model without breaking base contact.

If a model is ever without any of its base supported by terrain or the table, that model falls and suffers falling damage equal to half the distance it fell in inches (rounded down). It then continues any remaining portion of its movement as normal.

When resolving a **Walk** Action (see pg. 58), a model may move vertically along Climbable Terrain. To do so, it uses any amount of its movement distance to move vertically instead of horizontally. If a model moves in this way, it does not fall during this movement so long as it remains in base contact with the terrain. If the model's base is not supported by terrain or the table at the end of this movement, it falls as normal.

In addition to moving, both Push and Place effects are considered a type of movement and are treated as moving a model.

At no point can a model end any move with its base overlapping the base of another model, even if the model is able to move through the other model.

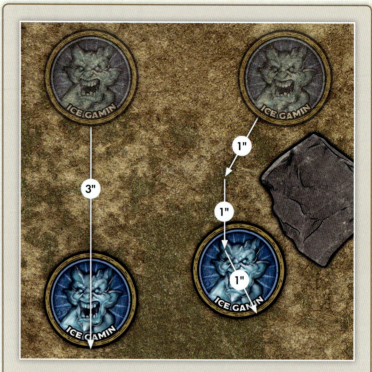

In this example, each Ice Gamin can move 3". The Ice Gamin on the left measures and moves straight 3". The Ice Gamin on the right divides the 3" up into 3 different 1" segments in order to move around the rock.

Neither Ice Gamin may move any part of their base more than the 3" they are moving.

In this example, Pandora uses a movement effect to move Rasputina 2" to the left, using all of the movement horizontally. As soon as Rasputina's base is no longer on terrain or the table, she falls and suffers damage equal to half the distance she fell (based the Height that she fell from), rounded down.

Since she fell a distance of 2, Rasputina suffers 1 damage.

THE TABLE

Push

If a movement effect indicates that it is a Push, the movement must be in a straight line and may not be broken up into smaller horizontal segments. All Pushing is horizontal (though models may change elevation if they Push horizontally along a staircase or hill; see pg. 75 for more details).

If a Pushed model encounters another model or Impassable Terrain during this movement, its movement is interrupted and stops.

Place

When an object is Placed, it is picked up and put down in a specific location as determined by the text of the effect creating the Place. The model must be Placed in a way so that the object is supported by either the table or terrain.

If the Place effect has a range, measure from the closest point of the base in the desired direction to place the object (do not take into account vertical distance), and place it anywhere within that range. If it cannot fit in the location, it cannot be placed and does not move (or count as moving).

If a model begins or ends a Place effect in terrain (pg. 72), it counts as having moved through that terrain.

Toward and Away

If something is moving "toward" an object, it must move toward the center of that object.

If something is moving "away" from an object, it must move away from the center of that object.

In both cases, unless that something is being Pushed, it will move around things that would impede its movement (such as terrain with the Impassable or Severe traits, as described on pg. 73), provided that doing so will get it as close or as far from the object as possible (as appropriate).

Something moving toward an object cannot move further from that object at any point during its movement, even if doing so would ultimately bring it closer to the object at the end of its movement.

Similarly, something moving away from an object cannot move closer to that object at any point during its movement, even if doing so would ultimately leave it further from the object at the end of its movement.

In this example, Pandora is placing within 2". She is picked up and placed anywhere within that range, ignoring everything in between.

In this example, Pandora is moving 2" away from Rasputina. She uses the center of her and Pandora's base and moves 2" to end as far away as possible.

If there had been a rock behind Pandora, she would have moved around it, as doing so would leave her further away than if she hadn't moved around it.

THE TABLE

LINE OF SIGHT

Line of Sight (LoS) is used regularly in the game and is determined using sight lines. It is a representation of something seeing something else on the table.

LoS is most often used to see if two models can see each other. LoS is needed for most attacks. Models always have LoS to themselves.

A sight line is an imaginary straight line between two points on the edges of two objects' bases. Sight lines are drawn from a top-down perspective.

To determine LoS, draw a series of sight lines between the two objects. Sight lines between objects are never drawn in such a way that they cross either object's base. If the objects are on different levels of the same terrain piece, sight lines cannot be drawn through the terrain piece's ceiling or floors.

If at least one of the sight lines between two objects is unblocked, the objects have LoS to each other. If all the sight lines are blocked, the two objects may not have LoS to each other. See Blocked Line of Sight on the next column for more details.

Blocked Line of Sight

Sight lines can be blocked in two ways: by models and by terrain.

Any sight lines that cross over a model's base might be blocked, depending upon that model's Size (see "Line of Sight and Size," pg. 53).

Sight lines can also be blocked by Blocking Terrain, if the Blocking Terrain is tall enough (see the Blocking Terrain Trait, pg. 73).

In the example below, the crates are terrain with the Height 2 and Blocking traits, so all of Rasputina's sight lines to Pandora are blocked. She does not have LoS to Pandora.

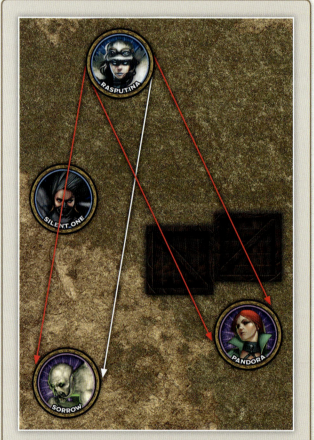

In this example, Rasputina is checking if she has LoS to the enemy models.

At least one sight line to the Sorrow is unblocked, so she has LoS to it. She only needs one such sight line to have LoS to the Sorrow.

Every sight line to Pandora is blocked because they cross terrain that has the Blocking trait. This means Rasputina and Pandora do not have LoS to each another.

In this example, Rasputina is drawing sight lines to the Sorrow. She draws a series of lines from the edge of her base to the Sorrow's, shown in white.

None of the sight lines should cross a model's bases, as shown in red.

THE TABLE

Dense Terrain

Dense Terrain can also block LoS in some circumstances. Sight lines that pass completely through Dense Terrain are blocked, but sight lines that only enter or leave Dense Terrain are not blocked. Models can see into and out of Dense Terrain, but they cannot see through it.

Line of Sight and Size

A model's Size can impact LoS.

When drawing LoS between two objects, any intervening models or terrain with a Size or Height that is lower than either of the two objects is ignored.

In this example, Ophelia is trying to draw LoS to Pandora, but Iggy is standing between them. Ophelia and Iggy are both Size 1, but Pandora is Size 2. Since Pandora is Size 2, all models or terrain with lower Size or Height (such as the Iggy are ignored when drawing LoS to her. Ophelia has LoS to Pandora.

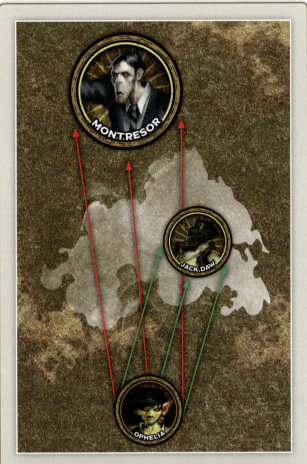

In this example, Jack Daw is in a stationary bank of sinister fog that has been deemed to be Concealing and Dense Terrain. Montresor is hanging further back, outside the fog.

Ophelia is trying to draw LoS to Jack Daw and Montresor. Her sight lines to Jack Daw enter the fog bank but do not leave it due to the Dense trait, so they are not blocked. She has LoS to Jack Daw (though he will have Concealment against any attacks she makes targeting him due to the fog's Concealing Terrain Trait).

Ophelia's sight lines to Montresor enter the fog bank and then leave it, so these sight lines are blocked due to the fog's Dense Trait. Since all of her sight lines are blocked, Ophelia does not have LoS to Montresor.

THE TABLE

Terrain with Height

If a model is standing on terrain with the Height Trait, it adds the Height of that terrain to its Size for the purposes of determining LoS.

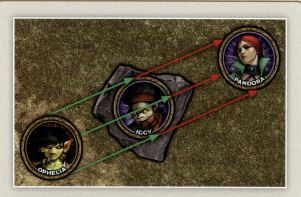

In this example, Ophelia is once again trying to draw LoS to Pandora. This time, however, Iggy is standing on a Height 1 rock, increasing his Size to 2 for the purposes of determining LoS. Since Ophelia is Height 1, the effective Height 2 Iggy blocks her LoS to the Height 2 Pandora.

Similarly, if a terrain piece with Height is atop another terrain piece with Height (most often because a terrain piece like an Ice Pillar was created atop a building's roof), their Heights are added together as described above for the purposes of determining LoS.

Shadow

Terrain that has both the Height and Blocking Traits casts a "Shadow," which is a catch-all term used to represent overhangs, sight angles, and places where models can crouch down to avoid being seen.

A terrain's Shadow extends out from the terrain a distance equal to the terrain's Height, to a maximum of 3″.

When drawing sight lines from one model to another, if either model is in the Shadow of terrain with Height equal to or greater than the Size of that model (even partially), any sight lines that pass through the terrain generating that Shadow are blocked (even if the terrain is being ignored due to its Height, as per the Line of Sight and Size rules on pg. 53).

When drawing sight lines, a model standing on terrain that is casting a Shadow ignores that terrain (and its Shadow) if any single sight line drawn between the two objects passes through 1″ or less of that terrain.

Models within a terrain's Shadow (even partially) have Cover against any ⌐ Actions that can draw one or more sight lines through that terrain.

In this example, Parker Barrows is standing atop a Height 3 piece of Blocking Terrain and is attempting to draw LoS to Dashel Barker.

Dashel is in the Shadow of terrain with a Height greater than her Size (which is 2), so any sight lines that pass through the terrain are blocked.

However, since Parker is standing on the terrain, he ignores the first 1" of that terrain when drawing sight lines to other models. This gives Parker LoS to Dashel, and he won't gain Cover against his ⌐ Actions.

THE TABLE

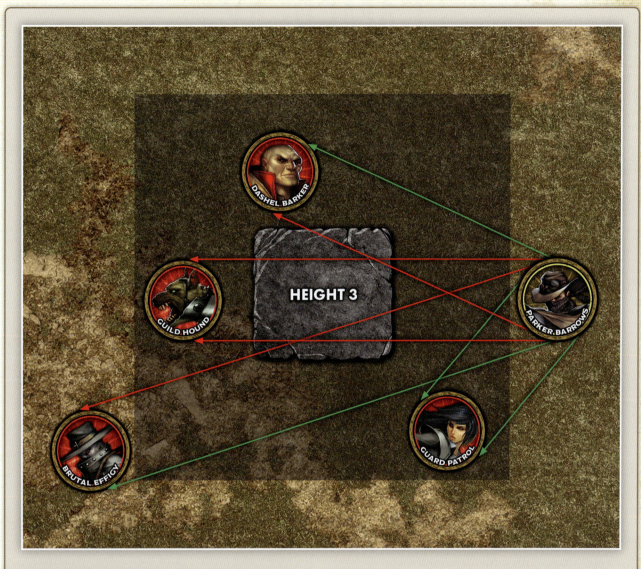

In this example, Parker Barrows is drawing LoS to the Guard Patrol. The Guard Patrol is entirely within the terrain's Shadow and the terrain's Height is greater than the Size of both Parker (Size 2) and the Guard Patrol (Size 2), so any sight lines that pass through the terrain are blocked. Parker has an unblocked sight line, so he has LoS to the Guard Patrol, but none of the sight lines actually pass through the terrain, so the Guard Patrol does not gain Cover against Parker's ⚔ Actions.

Dashel Barker is also in the terrain's Shadow. Parker has an unblocked sight line to Dashel, so he has LoS, but since one of the sight lines passes through the terrain, Dashel will have Cover against Parker's ⚔ Actions (but he would not have Cover against Dashel's ⚔ Actions, as he is not in the terrain's Shadow).

There is an unblocked sight line between Parker and the Brutal Effigy, so Parker has LoS. At least one sight line is blocked by the terrain, but because the Brutal Effigy is not within the terrain's Shadow, it does not receive Cover from Parker's ⚔ Actions.

Parker next tries to draw LoS to the Guild Hound. The Guild Hound is entirely within the terrain's Shadow, and the terrain's Height is greater than the Size of both Parker and the Guild Hound (Size 1), so any sight lines that pass through the terrain are blocked. Since Parker does not have any unblocked sight lines to the Guild Hound, he does not have LoS to it.

If the Guild Hound had been Size 4 (i.e., larger than the terrain), then Parker and the Guild Hound would have LoS to each other, since its size would be larger than the terrain. In this circumstance, the Guild Hound would have Cover from Parker's ⚔ Actions (since it's within the terrain's Shadow), but Parker would not have Cover against the Guild Hound's ⚔ Actions, since he is not within the Shadow.

GAMEPLAY

The goal in a game of Malifaux is to score more VP (Victory Points) than your opponent, which are based on the Encounter's Schemes and Strategies (see pg. 76 for more info on Encounters).

A game of Malifaux takes place over five Turns, which are each broken down into multiple Phases.

Turn Sequence

- **Start Phase**: Discard Cards, Draw Cards, Initiative Flip, Resolve Effects, Calculate Pass Tokens.
- **Activation Phase:** Pass, Select Model, Activation, Transfer Active Player.
- **End Phase**: Resolve Effects, Score VP, Check for End of Game, and Shuffle.

START PHASE

The Start Phase is made up of the five steps outlined below. Once the Start Phase is finished, proceed to the Activation Phase.

A. Discard Cards: Players may discard any cards from their Hand.

B. Draw Cards:
1. Players with fewer cards in hand than their maximum hand size (which is normally six) draw cards until they reach that number of cards.
2. Each player may spend a single Soulstone to draw two cards. After drawing these cards, the players must (as usual) discard down to their maximum hand size.

C. Initiative Flip:
1. Players simultaneously flip a card.
2. Players may Cheat Fate with a card from their hand, starting with the player with the lower flip (in a tie, the player with Initiative has the first opportunity to Cheat Fate).
3. The players add the number of Pass Tokens they possess to their total. The player with the highest value may choose which player has Initiative (Initiative lasts until another effect grants Initiative). If the values are tied, start again from the first step. Then, after Initiative has been determined, both players discard their Pass Tokens.

D. Resolve Effects: Resolve any effects that happen during the Start Phase, starting with the player with Initiative.

E. Calculate Pass Tokens: Count the number of models each Crew has in play. The Crew with fewer models gains a number of Pass Tokens equal to the difference.

> ### PASS TOKENS
>
> At the end of the Start Phase, count the number of models each Crew has in play. The player with fewer models gains Pass Tokens equal to the difference.
>
> During the Activation Phase, the Active player may discard a Pass Token in lieu of choosing a model to Activate. If they do so, the opponent then becomes the Active player and continues with the Activation Phase.
>
> In the Start Phase of the *next* Turn, after players have had an opportunity to Cheat Fate on their Initiative flip, each player adds the number of Pass Tokens they possess to their Initiative total and then discards all of their Pass Tokens.
>
> Some models may also be able to discard Pass Tokens for various effects, as described on their Stat or Upgrade cards.

GAMEPLAY

ACTIVATION PHASE

In this Phase, each player takes turns as the Active player, beginning with the player with Initiative. Proceed to the End Phase once every model has Activated this Turn.

A. Pass: The Active player may discard a Pass Token to skip to Step D, without Activating a model.

B. Select Model: The Active player chooses one of their models that has not yet Activated this Turn to Activate. No model may Activate more than once in a Turn. If the Active player does not have any more models to Activate, skip to Step D.

C. Activation: The chosen model Activates (it is now the Acting model) and follows the steps below.

1. **Start Activation:** Resolve any effects that happen at the start of a model's Activation.

2. **Taking Actions:** Models may take up to two Actions during their Activation, save for Leaders and Masters, who can take up to three Actions. This is referred to as a model's Action Limit. These Actions are resolved one at a time, with each Action fully resolving (including any Triggers) before the next Action begins (see Actions on pg. 58).

    If a model would gain or end **Fast**, **Slow**, or **Stunned** (pg. 65) during an Activation, the effects of the Condition come into effect immediately and are ignored as soon as the Condition has ended.

3. **End Activation:** Resolve any effects that happen at the end of a model's Activation. The model is considered to have Activated this Turn.

4. **Chain Activations:** Some effects can cause models to Activate after another model. If a model would Activate this way, immediately go back to the start of Step C. Players may not Activate more than two models in a row this way, unless they are Activated by the same effect.

D. Transfer Active Player: If there are still models left to Activate this Turn, the opponent becomes the Active player and starts at step A. Otherwise, proceed to the End Phase.

END PHASE

A. Resolve Effects: All effects that resolve during the End Phase resolve now. If there are multiple effects, follow the timing rules on page 70.

B. Score VP: Starting with the player with Initiative, Crews score Victory Points (VP) for objectives that score at the end of the Turn. A Strategy cannot score more than 4 total VP, and Schemes cannot score more than 2 VP each. No Victory Points can be scored on the first Turn.

All Victory Points in Malifaux are scored one at a time, completely resolving the scoring effect before moving onto the next scoring effect.

Points for Strategies are always scored before points for Schemes.

C. Check for End of Game: If it is Turn 5, the game ends at this time. If the game ends, score "end of game" Victory Points.

These "end of game" Victory Points are still considered to be scored during the Turn, so a player may not score the "end of game" Victory Points and the "reveal" Victory Points of a Scheme during the same turn.

D. Shuffle Discard Piles: This step is not used if the Encounter has ended. Players shuffle their Discard Piles back into their Fate Decks. Players should set aside their Control Hands so they do not accidentally shuffle their hand back into the deck as well.

Finally, the Turn ends, and play proceeds to the Start Phase of the next Turn.

CORE RULEBOOK • MALIFAUX THIRD EDITION

GAMEPLAY

ACTIONS

Models in Malifaux have a range of Actions they can perform. An example Action is listed below:

Attack Actions	RG	Stat	Rst	TN
↘ **Eldritch Blast**	⌐12"	5 🎯	Df	13 📖
Discard a card. Target suffers 2/3/4 damage.				

An Action's name is listed in bold on the left. The ↘ icon before its name indicates that it is a Bonus Action. Bonus Actions do not count against a model's Action limit, but a model can only declare one Bonus Action per Activation.

Range comes next, which may have an icon denoting its type (▨ is Melee, ⌐ is Projectile, ⑴ is Pulse, ◉ is Aura) and the range in inches, which is the maximum distance the Action can affect.

Any Action that requires a duel will have a Stat. This is what the model adds to the card it flips in the duel (in this case, 5). It may also have a Fate Modifier, which impacts the flip for that Action, and/or a suit, which is added to the model's final duel total.

Actions that involve duels have a Resist, a TN, or both. If the Action causes an opposed duel, it will list the stat the opponent uses to resist the duel here (usually **Df** or **Wp**).

An Action with a Resist is an Attack Action. An Action without a Resist is a Tactical Action.

If an Action has a TN value, that is listed next (in this case, the TN is 13 📖). For the Action to be successful, the model's duel total must reach this value or higher (including any listed suits). If an Action has both a Resist and a TN, the model must succeed on both aspects (equal or exceed the target's duel total and the TN value) to be successful.

Some Actions may have special requirements, costs, and/or additional effects, which are listed in *italics* before the Action's effects.

BONUS ACTIONS

Bonus Actions (denoted with the ↘ icon) are Actions that do not count against a model's Action limit. A model can only take one Bonus Action per Activation, unless the Action was generated by a Trigger.

General Actions

The Actions listed below are available to all models in the game.

Interact
Cannot be declared while engaged or if this model has taken the Disengage Action this Activation. Do one of the following: 1) Drop a Scheme Marker into base contact with this model and not within 4" of another friendly Scheme Marker, 2) remove all Scheme Markers in base contact with this model, or 3) resolve a specific rule that refers to an **Interact** Action.

Disengage
Can only be declared while engaged. One enemy model engaging this model (opponent's choice) may take a ▨ Action targeting this model; neither model can declare Triggers during this Action. After resolving the Attack (if any), this model pushes up to its **Mv** in inches. If the attack is successful, instead of its normal effects, reduce this model's Push distance by 2/4/6 inches (using the Accuracy Fate Modifier of the Action). This flip receives a ➕ for every other enemy model engaging this model.

Concentrate
Once per Activation. This model gains **Focused +1**.

Assist
Target other friendly model within 2" and LoS lowers the value of its **Burning**, **Distracted**, or **Injured** Condition by 1/2/3.

Walk
This model moves up to its Movement (**Mv**) in inches. This move cannot be used to leave an enemy model's engagement range.

Charge
Once per Activation. Cannot be declared while engaged. Push this model up to its **Mv** in inches. It may then take a ▨ Action that does not count against its Action limit.

> So what's the difference between Walking and Charging? Walking is your main way of moving your models. While it can't be used to get away from an enemy, it can be used to move around an enemy when you're engaged.
>
> Charging is your main way of getting your models into melee combat, as it lets them attack after they're Pushed (though you don't have to). It can also be used to rush past an enemy without engaging them. The downside? You can't Charge while engaged.

RESOLVING ACTIONS

Resolving Actions is a straightforward process. The model proceeds through the five steps below in order:

1. Declare the Action
2. Pay any Costs
3. Targeting
4. Perform Duels
5. Apply Results

Step 1: Declare the Action

Announce what Action the model is taking.

Step 2: Pay any Costs

If the Action has any costs in italics, they must be paid now, and are considered paid when declaring the Action. If the costs are not paid, the Action fails; skip steps 3, 4, and 5. Costs that reference an Action's target must instead be paid as part of declaring the target (step 3). Otherwise, the model cannot be targeted.

Step 3: Targeting

In addition to costs, special restrictions are also written in italics and restrict the Action in some way, such as limiting the Action to targeting Friendly models only, or non-Construct models only.

If the Action requires a target, the target must be declared at this step. The target must be within the Action's range as well as within LoS of the model taking the Action, unless specified otherwise. If an Action has no legal target, it fails; skip steps 4 and 5. A model may not target itself with an Attack Action.

If an Action requires a model to choose an object (model, marker, etc.) the object is not treated as being targeted and ignores any effects from targeting.

Unless otherwise mentioned, every Action with a target must target a single model.

Step 4: Perform Duels

If the Action requires a duel, the model now performs the duel (pg. 46). If the initiating model does not succeed on the duel, the Action fails and Step 5 of resolving an Action is not performed.

Some Actions have additional effects that affect an Action's duel (such as ignoring Concealment). These effects are listed next to the Action in italics.

If no duel was required, then the Action is automatically successful.

Step 5: Apply Results

The model performs the Action's effects, as stated on the card, in the order they are listed. If any of an Action's effects cannot be resolved, they are ignored.

A model is considered to be resolving an Action during every part of the "Resolving Actions" process. For instance, if a model was in Hazardous Terrain (pg. 73) during any part of the "Resolving Actions" process, the effects of the Hazardous Terrain are applied to the model after the Action resolves.

The most common effect of an Action is damage, which is explained on page 60.

Step 6: After Resolving

Any effects that happen after an Action is resolved, including any *After Resolving* and *After Succeeding* Triggers happen at this time. Remember: Triggers that do not specify a timing are assumed to be *After Succeeding* Triggers.

SPECIAL RESTRICTIONS

Some Actions or Triggers have various special restrictions that limit the Action/Trigger so that it can only be declared in specific circumstances. These effects (written in italics) can be complicated, such as *"This Action can only be taken while engaged."* Or they can be simple, such as *"Enemy only."*

Listed below are the basic restrictions and how they work, which can be put together in any combination:

Enemy only: This effect can only be declared if the target of this Action and the Attacking model are considered enemies.

Friendly only: This effect can only be declared if the target of this Action is a friendly model.

X only: This effect can only be declared if the target of this Action has the X Characteristic, Keyword, or Name.

Other model only: This effect can only be declared if the target of this Action is a model other than the model declaring the effect.

GAMEPLAY

ABILITIES

Models have a range of Abilities that affect how they function on the table. Abilities are found on the front of a model's Stat Card.

Most Abilities are passive, meaning that they are always in effect. Some Abilities, however, are active and create certain effects in reaction to other events on the table. When an active Ability goes into effect, resolve the effect step by step in the order it is listed on the Ability.

If a model gains a second instance of an Ability it already possesses (most often from an Upgrade), the second instance of the Ability has no effect unless the Ability has a value (such as **Armor +1**).

If an Ability has a value, then the values of that Ability's values with a "+" in front of them are combined together.

> **Example:** A model has "**Armor +1:** Reduce all damage suffered by this model by +1." If the model gains **Armor +1** from an Upgrade or other effect, the Abilities would combine to give it "**Armor +2:** Reduce all damage suffered by this model by +2."

DAMAGE

When a model suffers damage, it loses Health equal to the amount of damage it suffered. A model may not have its Health reduced below 0. If it would suffer damage that would bring its Health below 0, any additional damage is ignored. When a model reaches 0 Health, it is killed.

If a game effect references the amount of damage suffered, it is referring to the amount of damage suffered after damage reduction.

Damage can be inflicted as a static profile (such as 4) or as a variable profile (such as 2/3/4). If the damage profile is variable, a damage flip must be made.

Damage Flips

A damage flip is a variable flip (pg. 44) that determines how much damage a model suffers due to an effect. Damage flips are not a type of duel and are unaffected by game effects that reference duels. The most common modifier for damage flips is an Accuracy Fate Modifier.

Accuracy Fate Modifiers

Accuracy Fate Modifiers occur when there is a variable flip (often a damage flip) as the result of an opposed duel.

The Accuracy Fate Modifiers are determined by the differences in the final duel total based on the breakdown below:

- **Tied:** The damage flip will suffer ⊟⊟.
- **1 to 5:** The damage flip will suffer a ⊟.
- **6 to 10:** The damage flip won't have a modifier for accuracy.
- **11+:** The damage flip will receive a ⊞.

The result of the flip will determine whether the damage is Weak (0-5), Moderate (6-10), or Severe (11-14), as outlined in the variable flip rules (pg. 44). Like other flips, a player may Cheat Fate on their damage flips, but not if they have one or more ⊟ modifiers.

When flipping for damage, if a Joker is flipped or Cheated, it has the following effects:

> **Black Joker:** the damaged model suffers no damage and the Action does not generate any 🟢 (if applicable).
>
> **Red Joker:** the damaged model suffers the indicated Severe damage value +1.

Models that can use Soulstones can spend a single Soulstone before a damage flip is made against them to add a ⊟ to the damage flip.

Damage Reduction

Damage reduction always takes place after damage is determined, at which point the reduction amount is removed from the damage total. Irreducible damage ignores damage reduction from all game effects.

Reduction may not decrease the total damage amount below 1 unless otherwise stated (such as by using Soulstones).

When a model that can use Soulstones suffers damage, it may spend a Soulstone to reduce that damage. The model flips a card, which cannot be cheated, and reduces the damage it suffers by 1/2/3. This reduction occurs after all other reduction and can reduce damage to 0.

If a model suffers 0 damage, it is not considered to have suffered damage.

> ### ADDING DAMAGE
>
> Sometimes, an Action that normally doesn't deal damage will gain an effect that increases its damage by +1 (or more). If this happens, treat the original Action as dealing 0 damage (before any modifiers are added).

Healing

When a model Heals, it gains an amount of Health equal to the healing effect. A model's Health cannot exceed its maximum Health; if a Heal effect would cause it to exceed this limit, any additional Healing is ignored (as though it did not occur).

Markers and Killed Models

Sometimes, when a model is killed, it leaves behind a 30mm Marker to represent a husk of its former self, which can be used in various game effects.

After a model with the Living, Undead, or Beast Characteristic is killed, it Drops a Corpse Marker into base contact with itself.

After a model with the Construct Characteristic is killed, it Drops a Scrap Marker into base contact with itself.

If a model would drop multiple Markers this way, it only Drops one Marker, chosen by the model's controller.

For more information on Markers, see page 64.

Killed

Models are most often killed as a result of being reduced to 0 Health, but some game effects can instantly kill models regardless of their Health.

When a model is killed, any Healing effects or effects that result in the killed model being Replaced happen first, followed by any other effects that occur when, if, or after the model is killed. Then, the killed model Drops any Markers as a result of being killed and is removed from the game (including its Stat Card and Attached Upgrades). For more information on timing, see page 70.

Killed models are always considered to be killed by the model that generated the Action or Ability that killed them (as well as by that model's Crew). If a model is killed by another effect (such as a Condition or Hazardous Terrain), it is not considered to have been killed by any player, model, or Crew.

There are some game effects that can Heal a model after it has been killed. If a model is Healed after it was killed as a result of being reduced to 0 Health, it no longer counts as killed (and is not removed from the game). Any other effects that would happen as the result of the model being killed do not occur.

If a model was Healed after being killed by a game effect (as opposed to being reduced to 0 Health), then being Healed does not prevent it from being killed.

GAMEPLAY

FRIENDLY, ENEMY, & CONTROL

Friendly models, Markers, and terrain are those that have been hired into your Crew, and those Summoned, Dropped, or Created by your Crew.

Enemy models, Markers, and terrain are those that have been hired into the opponent's Crew, and those Summoned, Dropped, or Created by the opponent's Crew.

Every Ability, Action, and Trigger on a model's Stat Card and Attached Upgrades treats the use of "friendly" and "enemy" from its point of view.

Certain Actions and Abilities allow a player to control a model in an enemy's Crew. When this happens, the controlling player makes all decisions for the model, including flipping cards, Cheating Fate, declaring Actions, and so on.

> **Example:** A model has an Action that reads *"Target Pushes 3" toward the nearest other enemy model."* It successfully uses this Action on the opponent's model, so when resolving, the opponent's model Pushes 3" toward the nearest other model controlled by that opponent.

If the controlled model Cheats Fate, the controlling player must do so from their own Control Hand. If the controlled model uses a Soulstone or discards a card, Pass Token, or other resource, the controlling player must discard the appropriate Soulstone, card, Pass Token, etc. If the controlled model would gain a resource (cards, Pass Token, etc.), the controlling player gains that resource. If a controlled Action generates additional Actions, the controlling player controls the generated Action, as well.

Regardless of control, the model does not change which models it considers friendly and which it considers an enemy. Control changes who makes the decisions; it does not change the Crew to which the model belongs.

> Sometimes the best thing about being buddies is that you can get into a scuffle and walk away as friends. This is also the case in Malifaux. Models are free to attack other Friendly models.
>
> Sometimes you end up controlling an enemy model, via something like an Obey Action. You can still make that model attack its own Crew as there's nothing stopping Friendly models from attacking each other. But remember, no 🏆!

ENGAGEMENT

Every model has an engagement range based on the range of its longest 🗡 Action. If an enemy model is within a friendly model's engagement range and the friendly model has LoS to the enemy model, the friendly model is considered to be engaging the enemy model, and the enemy model is considered to be engaged by the friendly model.

If the friendly model has a longer engagement range than the enemy model, this could lead to situations where the friendly model is engaging the enemy model, but the enemy model is not engaging the friendly model (because the friendly model is not within its engagement range).

Models that do not have 🗡 Actions do not have engagement ranges.

Being engaged has five primary effects on models:

- Engaged models cannot take 🏹 Actions.
- Engaged models cannot take the **Interact** Action.
- Engaged models cannot leave an enemy model's engagement range with a **Walk** Action.
- Engaged models cannot take the **Charge** Action.
- Targeting engaged or engaging models with 🏹 Actions incurs Friendly Fire.

Friendly Fire

When a model performs a Projectile (🏹) Action targeting an engaged or engaging model, the Action suffers a ⊟ to its duel.

While not common, some models are able to take 🏹 Actions while engaged. If a model does so, it is not considered engaging (or engaged by) the target for the purposes of Friendly Fire.

GAMEPLAY

SOULSTONES

Some models have the ability to use powerful resources called Soulstones, which are stored in its Soulstone Pool, an area beside the game table. As long as there are Soulstones in your Crew's Soulstone Pool, these models may spend them for various bonuses. When a Soulstone is spent, it is discarded from that player's Soulstone Pool and cannot be used again. A model can only use one Soulstone at a time for any game effect.

By default, only two types of models can use Soulstones: Masters and Henchmen.

Soulstones can be used in the following ways:

Draw Cards: During the Draw Phase, each player may spend a Soulstone to draw two cards and must then (as usual) discard down to their maximum hand size. This can be done even if the player does not have a model that can use Soulstones remaining in its Crew.

Enhance a Duel: Before any cards are flipped in a duel, a model that can use Soulstones may spend a single Soulstone to add a ✚ to its flip or to add a suit of its choice to its final duel total. If both models involved in the duel can use Soulstones, the attacker declares its Soulstone use (or lack of use) first.

Block Damage: A model that can use Soulstones can spend a single Soulstone before a damage flip is made against it to add a ⊟ to that damage flip.

Reduce Damage: After damage is suffered by a model that can use Soulstones, it may spend a Soulstone to reduce that damage. The model flips a card, which can't be cheated, and reduces the damage it suffers by 1/2/3. This reduction occurs after all other reduction and can reduce damage to 0.

> Sometimes during a game you might ask yourself, "Can this flip be Cheated?" Yes, probably. There are two things that prohibit the ability to Cheat, though: ⊟ Modifiers and effects that specifically say otherwise. Everything else is fair game (or *un*fair game, am I right?).

TOKENS

Malifaux uses Tokens to track various things. When a Crew gains a Token (such as a Pass Token), that Token is placed near the table in a place where its Crew will remember it.

When a model gains a Token, it has that Token for the rest of the game unless the Token is removed by another effect.

Tokens have no effect on their own but are often referenced by the Actions and Abilities of models.

Tokens do not need to be tracked with a physical token. If a player prefers, they may instead track tokens using any other method (dice, writing on stat cards, tracking cards), but its representation on the table must be visibly apparent to all players.

GAMEPLAY

MARKERS

Markers are Dropped on the table during an Encounter to represent objectives or other game events based on the Marker's description.

A Marker's default base size is 30mm, unless otherwise noted in the Marker's description. All Markers have the following common rules:

- Unless otherwise noted, Markers do not count as terrain and have no vertical distance (i.e., Height or Size). Markers that count as terrain will have one or more Terrain Traits (such as a Concealing, Severe Dust Cloud Marker).

- If terrain would be created or moved on top of a Marker, the Marker is placed on top of the terrain without changing the Marker's position on the table's horizontal surface (the Marker moves vertically upward). If a Marker is moved off an elevated surface, it falls just like a model.

- Models can usually move over and stop on Markers. A Marker is ignored for movement purposes unless it possesses one or more Terrain Traits (such as Hazardous, Severe, etc.).

- Markers cannot be moved from their position on the table or destroyed unless an effect states otherwise.

- When a model Drops a Marker, it is friendly to the Crew controlling the model that Dropped it.

- Markers do not block LoS (unless they have the Blocking Trait).

- When drawing LoS to a Marker, the Marker is treated as a model with Size 0, unless the Marker has the Height Terrain Trait, in which case its Size is equal to its Height.

Sometimes, two Markers will overlap or be on top of each other. When this happens, both Markers have their full effect; it doesn't matter which one is on top of the other.

If a model is standing perfectly atop a Marker with the same base size (such as a model on a 30mm base standing perfectly atop a 30mm Marker), it does not block sight lines drawn to that Marker.

Drop and Create

When a Marker is added to the table, it can be either Dropped or Created.

If a Marker is Dropped, it is simply put on the table in the indicated location without any further game effects; this is not considered moving the Marker. It can be put into base contact or even under a model's base without issue. If an Impassable Marker is Dropped, it is always treated as being Created instead.

If a Marker is Created, it is treated as Dropped, with the following additional rules described below:

- Created Markers can overlap non-Impassable terrain, but they cannot overlap other Markers.

- Created Markers cannot be put into base contact with any models except for the model creating them. Impassable Markers cannot be Created in such a way that their base overlaps the base of the model creating them.

Scheme Markers

Scheme Markers are primarily Dropped or removed by using the **Interact** Action (pg. 58).

Scheme Markers do not do anything on their own but are often used in conjunction with the Abilities and Actions of various models. They are also used to score certain Schemes (pg. 82).

Strategy Markers

Strategy Markers are often put on the table by the Strategy or the players throughout the game.

Strategy Markers cannot be affected by the effects of models (such as moving, removing, or targeting) except by those effects which are specifically called out in the Strategy.

GAMEPLAY

CONDITIONS

Conditions are ongoing effects that models may receive during the game. They impact how the model functions on the table in a variety of ways.

A model can only have one instance of each Condition at a time. If a Condition is canceled by another Condition, both Conditions are immediately removed from the model in question.

Some Conditions have an associated value, such as **Burning +1**. If a model with such a Condition gains another instance of that same Condition, the value of the gained Condition is added to the model's existing value for that Condition to create a single Condition. For example, if a model with **Burning +2** gains **Burning +1**, the two Conditions are combined into **Burning +3**.

Some game effects cause models to suffer damage from a Condition. Damage suffered this way is affected by any effects referring to the Condition.

If an Action would kill a model from damage suffered from a Condition (such as an Action that states "Target suffers 2 damage from the Burning Condition"), the model taking the Action is considered to have killed the model.

A Condition with a value cannot have that value reduced below 0. When the value of a Condition reaches 0 or during the timing specified by that Condition, the Condition ends (as stated below).

Malifaux Conditions (End of Activation)

- **Fast:** The number of Actions this model can declare during its Activation is increased by one, to a maximum of three. End this Condition at the end of this model's Activation. Canceled by **Slow**.

- **Slow:** The number of Actions this model can declare during its Activation is decreased by one. End this Condition at the end of this model's Activation. Canceled by **Fast**.

- **Staggered:** This model suffers -2 **Mv** and cannot be moved by the effects of other friendly models. End this Condition at the end of this model's Activation.

- **Stunned:** This model cannot declare Triggers and its Bonus Actions (✤) count against its Action limit. End this Condition at the end of this model's Activation.

Malifaux Conditions (End Phase)

- **Adversary (X):** Models with the "X" Keyword, Characteristic, or Name receive a ➕ to Attack Actions targeting this model. A model cannot benefit from the **Adversary** Condition more than once per Attack Action. During the End Phase, end this Condition.

- **Shielded +X:** Reduce damage suffered by this model by 1, to a minimum of 0. Each time this Condition reduces damage, its value is lowered by one. During the End Phase, end this Condition.

- **Injured +X:** This model suffers -X **Df** and **Wp**. During the End Phase, end this Condition.

Malifaux Conditions (Special)

- **Burning +X:** During the End Phase, this model suffers 1 damage, plus 1 additional damage for every 3 points of **Burning** beyond the first that it possesses.

- **Distracted +X:** This model's Actions that target an enemy model suffer a ➖ to their duel. After resolving such an Action, the value of this Condition is lowered by one.

- **Focused +X:** Before performing an opposed duel, this model may lower the value of this Condition by one to receive a ➕ to the duel (and any resulting damage flip this model makes).

- **Poison +X:** During the End Phase, this model suffers 1 damage, plus 1 additional damage for every 3 points of **Poison** beyond the first that it possesses. Then, it lowers the value of this Condition by one.

ASSIST

Remember: every model has access to the following Action allowing them to remove debilitating Conditions from other models:

Assist
Target other friendly model within 2″ and LoS lowers the value of its **Burning**, **Distracted**, or **Injured** Condition by 1/2/3.

CORE RULEBOOK • MALIFAUX THIRD EDITION   65

GAMEPLAY

AREA EFFECTS

Area effects are game effects that influence an area of the table that is larger than a single model. Some are lasting while others are temporary.

There are four different area effects in Malifaux.

Blasts ☁

Some damage profiles contain a Blast icon (☁). This represents an Attack that affects the target and any models near the target. A ☁ is represented by a 50mm base.

A ☁ is Dropped by the Active player into base contact with the target. If more than one ☁ is Dropped (i.e., if multiple ☁ are shown), each additional ☁ must be Dropped into base contact with at least one other ☁ (instead of the target). A ☁ is assumed to extend 1″ vertically above and below the target's base (and thus may come into base contact with models that are slightly above or below the target).

All models, except the original target, whose bases are in base contact with one or more ☁ take damage that is one step lower than the damage suffered by the original target (e.g., if the target took Severe damage, the ☁ will do Moderate damage). If the original target suffered Weak damage, any resulting ☁ deal 1 damage.

The damage a model suffers from a ☁ is unaffected by effects that increase the damage the original target suffered from the attack. Attack Actions that target friendly models do not generate ☁.

In this example, Iggy has just been hit by Rasputina's **Winter's Strike** Action, which has Iggy suffer 2/3☁/4☁☁ damage. When resolving the Action, Rasputina flipped Severe on her damage flip, so Iggy suffers 4 damage and Rasputina Drops two Blast Markers; one touching Iggy, the other touching the previously Dropped Blast Marker, but also touching Pandora, so Pandora suffers 3 damage.

Auras ◉

The Aura icon (◉) means the Action or Ability affects an area around the object that has the Aura. An Aura extends out in all directions from an object a number of inches equal to the listed distance in inches, as measured from the edge of the object's base. For example, ◉3 means that everything within 3″ and LoS of the object is affected by the Aura.

Auras are lasting effects that move with the object as it moves. All models inside the Aura's area, including what is generating the Aura, are affected by the Aura as long as they stay inside the area and remain in LoS of the generating object. The "affected model" in these instances is whatever model experiences some change in game state.

Auras are not cumulative. If a model would be affected by multiple Auras of the same name (i.e., if the Aura would change its game state in some way), then it is only affected by one such Aura of its controller's choice.

> In this example, Jakob Lynch has the Hold 'Em Ability, which reads: "After an enemy model within ◉6 Cheats Fate, it suffers 1 damage after resolving the current Action or Ability."
>
> If an enemy model within 6" and LoS of Jakob Lynch Cheats Fate, then the enemy model is affected by Jakob Lynch's Hold 'Em Ability and suffers 1 damage after resolving the current Action or Ability. If there were multiple friendly models with Hold 'Em Ability within 6" and LoS of the enemy model, it would still only suffer 1 damage, since it can only be affected by one Aura of the same name.
>
> Example: Bushwhackers have the Scamper Ability, which reads: "After an enemy model within ◉6 Cheats Fate, this model may Push up to 2" in any direction after resolving the current Action or Ability."
>
> If an enemy model Cheats Fate within 6" and LoS of multiple Bushwhackers, each such Bushwhacker could Push up to 2", as they are the models affected by the Aura (i.e., the models experiencing a change in their game state).

GAMEPLAY

Pulses (✺)

The Pulse icon ((✺)) means the Action or Ability affects an area around the object that has created the Pulse. A Pulse always extends out in all directions from an object a number of inches equal to the Pulse's effect, as measured from the edge of the object's base.

Pulses are immediate 'burst' effects that have no game effect after they are resolved.

All models inside the Pulse's area or overlapping the object generating the Pulse, excluding the object that created the Pulse, are affected by the Pulse as long as they are in the generating object's LoS.

Shockwaves

Shockwaves Drop a 30mm Shockwave Marker on the table within range and LoS. When the Shockwave Action is fully resolved, the Marker is removed. Below is an example Shockwave.

Attack Actions	Rg	Stat	Rst	TN
Lightning Strike	8"	7	*	13
Shockwave 1, Mv 13, Damage 2.				

The Dropped Marker generates a (✺) equal to the Shockwave's value. This **Lightning Strike** Action generates a (✺)1 from the Dropped Shockwave Marker.

Any model that the Marker touches or that is affected by the (✺) must pass the simple duel noted in the Shockwave or suffer its effects. Both the simple duel and the penalty for failure are listed after the Shockwave value.

If a model would be affected by multiple Shockwave Markers Dropped by the same Action, it only resolves the effects of the Shockwave once.

Shockwaves are unaffected by Cover and Concealment.

MATH

Sometimes the game will require you to do some math. If you need to, the math should be applied in the following order: Multiply, Divide, Add, and then Subtract.

In all cases where you are dividing any number but a movement distance, you will need to round any fractions. In these cases, always round the sum up to the nearest whole number.

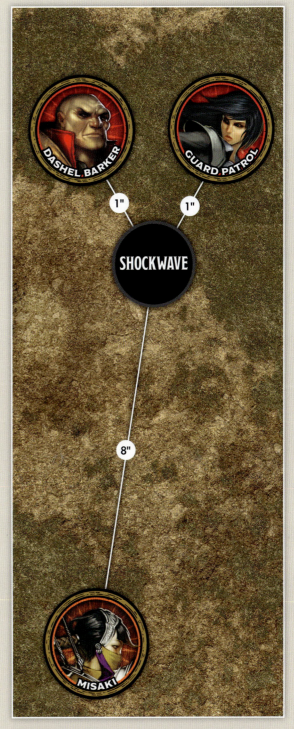

In this example, Misaki has taken the **Lightning Strike** Action. After succeeding at the Action's TN 13 duel (using her stat of 7). She then Drops a Shockwave Marker within 8" of herself. As they are both within 1" and LoS of the Shockwave Marker ((✺)1), Dashel Barker and the Guard Patrol must each pass a TN 13 **Mv** duel or suffer 2 damage.

GAMEPLAY

REPLACE

Some game effects Replace one model with another. When this occurs, follow the steps below.

1. Place the new model into base contact with the original. If it cannot fit, or if the new model cannot be added due to model limits or because the original model is Buried, the Replace effect is canceled.

2. The new model's Health is set to the original model's Health or to its maximum Health, whichever is lower. If the effect that Replaced the model Heals the new model, the new model Heals at this point.

3. If the original model had any Conditions or Tokens, the new model gains those Conditions at the same value (if any) and all Tokens. These Conditions, if gained during the End Phase, do not resolve their effects. Any Summon Upgrades Attached to the original model are Attached to the new model; all other Upgrades are discarded.

4. If the new and original models belong to the same Crew, the new model becomes the target of any effects that targeted or chose the original model, such as Schemes, Leader designation, or lasting game effects. The new model is always considered a legal target for those effects.

5. Remove the original model from the game. If the new and original models do not belong to the same Crew, the original model is considered to be killed. No game effects (such as placing Markers or scoring points) occur from the original model being removed.

6. If the new model is at 0 Health, it is killed.

7. If the original model was Replaced during its Activation, the new model continues the Activation using any remaining Actions. If the original model has already finished its Activation for the Turn, the new model is also considered to have Activated this Turn.

One model may also be Replaced by multiple models. If this happens, each new models must be placed into base contact with the original model. Resolve step 2 individually for each new model, then choose a single model for steps 3 and 4. If this happened during the original model's Activation, choose one new model to continue the Activation as in step 7 (the other models are not considered to have Activated).

If multiple models would be Replaced with one model, the new model is placed into base contact with any of the original models. Add the Health of the original models together for step 2. For step 3, the new model gains the highest value of every Condition on the original models (as well as every Condition without a value). In step 5, every original model is removed from the game. In step 7, if one of the original models was Replaced during its Activation, the new model continues that model's Activation.

If a model is affected by multiple Replace effects at the same time, its controller chooses one Replace effect to resolve and ignores the rest.

SUMMONING

Some Actions and Abilities can Summon a model. Summoning places a brand new model (specified by the Summoning effect) into play, adding the model to a player's existing Crew. After a model is Summoned in a Crew, the opposing Crew gains a Pass Token.

Summoned models are not hired at the start of an Encounter.

Summoned models are placed into base contact and within LoS of the model whose Action or Ability Summoned them unless the effect states otherwise. If it is not possible to place a Summoned model legally, the Summoned model is not added to the game.

The Summoned model is considered a part of the Crew of the model that Summoned it and is treated as a normal model in the Crew for the rest of the game.

Many Summoning effects require an Upgrade to be Attached to a model that is being Summoned. If the Upgrade cannot be Attached to the model (from the Upgrade's Limitations), the Summoned model is not added to the game.

Summoned models cannot take the **Interact** Action during the Turn they were Summoned.

MODEL LIMITS

Players cannot use Summon or Replace effects to add a model that is already in their Crew to their Crew. The only exception to this are models that have a number noted after their station Characteristic (i.e. **Minion (3)**).

If a Summoning or Replace effect would add a model that would take a player over this limit, the model is simply not added to the game.

BURY

Some effects Bury a model. Buried models are removed from the table, though they are still considered to be in play. While Buried models still Activate, they cannot take Actions.

Buried models cannot be the target of any Actions or Abilities that do not specifically target Buried models. These Actions ignore all game effects relating to the position of the Buried model, such as range, LoS, ⊙, (ⱡ), moving the Buried model, etc.

A Buried model can only be returned to the table via an Unbury effect. When Unburying a model, the controller of the Unbury effect places the model back on the table as described by the effect. If the model cannot be Placed, the owner of the model instead places it anywhere inside their Deployment Zone.

If a model is killed while Buried, it is removed from the game without placing any Markers. If a model is Buried when the game ends, it is killed.

Buried models cannot be Buried. If a Buried model would be Buried by a game effect, it ignores that game effect.

Models that are not Buried ignore any effects that would cause them to Unbury.

THE RULE OF INTENT

Occasionally in Malifaux, models may be moved in a way that they are obstructed by real-life obstacles, such that while the move is perfectly legal, it is physically impossible to perform. For example: moving two very large models into base contact when base contact between them may be obstructed by their sculpts.

This rule may also be used to declare intent when moving exact distances, such as moving a model so it is exactly 4″ away from another model, where measuring such a distance is either difficult or too time consuming.

Though it should only be used in scenarios with no other options, players may still move models this way by declaring their intent to their opponent first. The moving model must be moved to the closest possible position so that it is readily apparent of the intended position. All game effects, such as measuring distances, should be done from the intended position of the model.

"ONCE PER" EFFECTS

A model can only take an Action or Ability that is once per Activation once during an Activation.

A model can only take an Action or Ability that is once per Turn once on any given Turn.

These limitations are all by Action (or Ability) and model, so a given model could, for example, take multiple once per Activation effects so long as they were on different Actions or Abilities. Additionally, multiple models that have the same Action (or Ability) with a once per Activation can each use that effect once per Activation.

Some of these effects have additional modifiers, such as being limited to targeting a specific model once per Activation. These work the same way, with the specific limitations mentioned.

"THIS OR THAT" CHOICES

Some effects within the game provide a model with a choice, such as "discard a card or gain **Stunned**." In cases such as this, the model making the choice may choose either option, provided they have the capability to resolve that option. In the case above, if the model had no cards in its Control Hand, it could not choose to discard a card; if the model already had the **Stunned** Condition (or could not gain it for some reason), it could not choose to gain **Stunned**. If a model cannot resolve either option, the effect is ignored.

Many effects within Malifaux have a model perform a duel to avoid a negative effect (such as damage or gaining a Condition). In these cases, the affected model must attempt the duel, and should they fail, they suffer the effects of that duel.

Choosing to Suffer Damage

Some models in Malifaux may generate effects that require them to suffer damage, such as the cost of an Action, or an Ability that may be used by suffering damage. A model can never choose to suffer damage this way if that damage would reduce their Health to 0 or below.

GAMEPLAY

TIMING

Sometimes, many effects are happening at, or near, the same times. If there is any confusion on timing, the following two pages provide a detailed breakdown.

Ability Timing

Most Abilities are passive and always in effect, but some occur as a result of another game effect. In these cases, the Ability will use the word "After." These Abilities happen after the effect in question is resolved.

Damage Timing

When a model suffers damage, it follows the timing structure below. If multiple models suffer damage at the same time (such as from a Shockwave or Blast), resolve each step below on every model being damaged before moving to the next step.

1. If the model being damaged can use Soulstones, it may spend one here to give the damage flip a ⊟.

2. If there is a variable damage profile, flip for damage (including any Accuracy Fate Modifiers). Any "when resolving" Triggers that increase or add damage resolve at this point.

3. Apply damage reduction to incoming damage. Soulstone users can spend Soulstones to Reduce Damage. Any "when resolving" Triggers that reduce damage resolve at this point.

4. The model lowers its Health by an amount equal to the final damage amount.

5. Any effects that happen after a model is damaged or after a model is reduced to a specific Health, resolve at this point.

6. If a model is at 0 Health, it is killed, then resolve the following effects:

    a. Resolve any effects that would Heal or Replace the killed model. If this effect would bring the model above 0 Health, it is no longer killed.

    b. Resolve any *After killing* Triggers.

    c. Any effects that resolve after the model is killed (such as placing Corpse or Scrap Markers) resolve at this point.

    d. The killed model (its model, Stat Card, and any Upgrades) is removed from the game.

SEQUENTIAL EFFECTS

Sometimes, an effect will create additional effects as it resolves.

In these cases, fully resolve the initial effect before moving onto any additional effect. Additional effects are then resolved in the order they were generated, after any effects which had been previously generated have resolved.

Simultaneous Effects

Occasionally, an effect will generate multiple effects that occur at the same time. If this happens, they are resolved in the following order:

1. The Active player (or the player with Initiative, if there is no Active player) chooses one of their models with one or more unresolved effects and resolves those effects in whatever order they wish. Then, that player chooses another of their models with unresolved effects and resolves those effects in the same way, continuing in this manner until the player no longer has models with unresolved effects. When an effect resolves, the entire effect resolves (even if it also affects a model controlled by the non-Active player).

2. The non-Active player resolves any unresolved effects affecting their models, as described above.

3. Any remaining unresolved effects are resolved in an order determined by the Active player (or the player with Initiative, if there is no Active player).

ACTIONS GENERATED BY EFFECTS

Many effects in Malifaux, (such as Actions, Abilities, and Triggers) can cause a model to take an Action.

When this happens, the new Action is always resolved after the previous Action is completely resolved, including any "After Resolving" effects, but before any other new Action can be taken.

Actions generated in this way follow the normal sequence for Actions and do not count against a model's Action limit.

GAMEPLAY

DETAILED TIMING

START PHASE
A. Discard Cards: Both players may discard any unwanted cards.
B. Draw Cards: Each player draws up to their maximum hand size. Once complete, each player may spend a Soulstone to draw two cards (player with Initiative decides first).
C. Initiative Flip: Both players flip a card, which may be Cheated. The player with Initiative Cheats first in the case of ties. Players increase their totals by the number of Pass Tokens they possess and then discard their Pass Tokens.
D. Resolve Effects: Resolve any effects that happen during the Start Phase.
E. Calculate Pass Tokens: Count up the number of models controlled by both players. The player with fewer models in play gains Pass Tokens equal to the difference.

ACTIVATION PHASE
A. Decide to Pass: The Active player may discard a Pass Token to skip to Step D.
B. Select Model: The Active player Activates a friendly model that has not yet Activated this Turn.
C. Activation
  1. **Start Activation:** Resolve effects that happen at the start of a model's Activation.
  2. **Take Actions:** Most models can take two Actions. Leaders/Masters can take three Actions.
    a. Declare Action.
    b. Pay any Costs.
    c. Declare Target.
    d. Perform Duels.
      I. Modify The Duel with Soulstones, Abilities, or other game effects (Attacking model first).
      II. Flip Fate Cards (both players flip cards then choose a card).
      III. Cheat Fate (player with lowest total first).
      IV. Determine Duel Total.
      V. Declare Triggers (Active player first).
        i. *Immediately* Triggers occur.
      VI. Determine Outcome (if the Acting model's duel failed, the Action ends without resolving its effects. Skip Step e and move to Step f).
    e. Resolve effects in the order presented on the card, including any *When Resolving* Triggers. Damage timing can be found on page 70. If the target is killed, resolve any effects such as "After this model is killed" and any *After killing* Triggers.
    f. Anything that happens after an Action is resolved, including any *After Resolving* and *After Succeeding* Triggers. Remember: Triggers that do not specify a timing are assumed to be *After Succeeding* Triggers.
  3. **End Activation:** Resolve effects that happen at the end of a model's Activation. The model counts as having Activated this Turn.
  4. **Chain Activations:** Resolve any Chain Activations generated from an effect during this Activation.
D. Transfer Active Player: If there are still models left to Activate this Turn, the opponent becomes the Active player.

END PHASE
A. Resolve Effects: All "Until the End Phase" effects end, followed by "During the End Phase" effects being resolved.
B. Score VP: Strategies are scored first, then Schemes. If multiple players and/or Schemes are scoring, the player with Initiative determines the scoring order. No VP is scored on the first Turn.
C. Check for End of Game: as described on page 57. If the game ends, score "end of game" VP.
D. Shuffle Discard Piles: Each player shuffles their Discard Piles back into their Fate Decks.

If multiple Actions are generated, they are queued and resolved one at a time in the order they were generated (whichever happened first or was listed first on the card). If an Action in a queue generates an Action, that Action happens before moving to the next Action in the queue.

TERRAIN

TERRAIN

The different scenery used on the table is called terrain (but the table itself is not considered terrain). Terrain adds tactical dimensions to the battle by making some locations more ideal than others and creating obstacles for models to deal with.

Every terrain piece has one or more traits that determine how it interacts with models. For terrain of particularly large or complex pieces of terrain, it makes sense to assign traits to individual elements or smaller areas of that terrain.

Any time a model's base is overlapping terrain, it is said to be in that terrain. If a model's base is touching terrain (either overlapping or directly next to the terrain), that model is within 0″ of that terrain.

A list of Terrain Traits can be found on page 73.

HAZARDOUS MARKERS

Some game effects are capable of creating Markers with the Hazardous Trait.

All Markers with the same name (i.e., Pyre Markers, Pit Trap Markers, etc.) count as the same piece of terrain for the purposes of the Hazardous Terrain Trait.

Thus, if a model was Pushed through three Pyre Markers and a single Pit Trap Marker, it would suffer the effects of moving through a single Pyre Marker and a single Pit Trap Marker.

MOVING TERRAIN MARKERS

Some effects are capable of moving Markers with Terrain Traits, such as a Hazardous Pyre Marker or an Impassable Ice Pillar Marker.

When a Terrain Marker with the Climbable or Impassable Terrain Trait moves, it is treated as if it were a model (and thus it can move across the top of Climbable Terrain but cannot move through Impassable Terrain or models).

When other Terrain Markers move into base contact with a model or other object, their movement is not stopped by the object.

COVER & CONCEALMENT

Certain Terrain Traits and game effects grant Cover and/or Concealment.

Cover
When a model with Cover is the target of a ⌐ Action, it gains +1 **Df** and imposes a ⊟ on any damage flips against it.

Concealment
When a model with Concealment is targeted by a non-⚔ Attack Action, the Action's duel gains a ⊟.

> Cover and Concealment are pretty similar terms that mean two different things in Malifaux. Let's go over some of their differences:
>
> First, Cover isn't a Terrain Trait, but rather, the effects of Cover are generated by the Shadow rule and other game effects like Bodyguard.
>
> On the other hand, Concealment comes directly from Concealing Terrain and other game effects that generate Concealment like Vent Steam.
>
> Second, with Cover, you have to be near the object you're hiding behind whereas you don't necessarily have to with Concealment.
>
> I'd say that just about *covers* it.

TERRAIN

Terrain Traits

- **Blocking:** Terrain with the Blocking Trait cannot be seen through, and therefore it blocks LoS if the Height of the terrain is equal to or greater than the Size of the models attempting to draw sight lines through it. Terrain with the Blocking and Height Traits generates a Shadow (pg. 54).

- **Climbable:** Models may not move through Climbable Terrain, but they may move across its top (often a roof) and may move vertically up and down along its sides. Other than its top, all other portions of Climbable terrain are treated as Impassable.

- **Concealing:** If a sight line drawn to a model passes through Concealing Terrain, that model has Concealment. When drawing sight lines, a model in Concealing Terrain may ignore that terrain's Concealing trait if any single sight line drawn between the two objects passes through 1″ or less of that terrain. Most fog banks count as Concealing Terrain.

- **Dense:** LoS can be drawn into or out of Dense Terrain but not through it. Most woods count as Dense Terrain.

- **Destructible:** Models within 1″ of a piece of Destructible Terrain may take an Action to destroy that Destructible Terrain and remove it from the table. If a model is standing on Destructible Terrain when it is destroyed, that model falls.

- **Hazardous Terrain:** After a model moves through or resolves one of its Actions while in Hazardous Terrain, it suffers the effects of the Hazardous Terrain after the current Action or Ability is resolved (to a maximum of once per Action or Ability). Most of the time, Hazardous Terrain will give a Condition to a model, such as Hazardous Terrain (**Burning +1**) or Hazardous Terrain (**Poison +1**). If the Hazardous Terrain does not mention a Condition in its description, the model simply suffers 1 damage.

  - If a Hazardous Terrain Marker is moved, all models the Marker came into base contact with during the move, suffer the effects of the Hazardous Terrain. The model moving the Marker may choose to ignore the Hazardous effects of the moved Marker.

- **Height X (or Ht X):** Terrain with the Height Trait has a vertical component that is relevant to the game. Height primarily comes into play when determining LoS (pg. 52). Terrain with the Height and Blocking Traits generates a Shadow (pg. 54).

- **Impassable:** Models and Markers cannot move through Impassable Terrain, which often includes solid objects, such as Ice Pillars. Objects cannot be Dropped or placed overlapping Impassable Terrain.

- **Severe:** Non-Place movement effects are reduced by half while any part of a model's base is in Severe Terrain. If a model moves out of Severe Terrain, it continues the rest of its movement at its normal (non-halved) rate.

COMPLICATED TERRAIN

Occasionally, players might find themselves playing on a table that has one or more pieces of strangely shaped or abnormally large terrain pieces. In these circumstances, the players should ensure that the parameters of each piece of terrain are properly defined during the "Place and Define Terrain" step of Encounter Setup (pg. 76).

Sometimes, it can be useful to break complicated terrain pieces into multiple terrain pieces. For example, a terrain piece consisting of two buildings connected by a series of narrow planks might be more easily defined as two Buildings connected by multiple Bridges.

UNAFFECTED BY TERRAIN

Some models are unaffected by certain types of terrain or terrain Markers. If a model is unaffected by a terrain trait, it ignores that trait for game purposes:

Severe: The model does not suffer the movement penalty of Severe Terrain.

Hazardous: The model does not suffer the effects of the Hazardous Terrain.

Concealment: This model ignores the Concealing Trait when drawing LoS.

TERRAIN

Terrain Examples
Here are some common types of terrain that can be found in Malifaux.

Barbed Wire
Some parts of Malifaux have been cordoned off with barbed wire. It serves as more of a deterrent to movement than an actual impediment.

Barbed Wire counts as Hazardous Terrain.

Bridge
A Bridge is an elevated terrain piece that connects two locations while allowing models to pass beneath it, such as the eponymous bridge or a few planks connecting one building's roof to another.

Bridges can be divided into two sections: Walkways and Archways.

Archways: Archways are the open section beneath a Bridge that allows a model to move underneath the Bridge.

Archways are Height X Terrain, where X is equal to the Archway's Height in inches (rounded down). While many Archways are significantly curved, the Height of an Archway should stay consistent across the entire length of an Archway. This area is not Blocking or Impassable, so models can move freely underneath a Bridge in its Archway.

Walkways: Walkways are the solid portion of a bridge that allow models to pass over the bridge.

Walkways are Height X, where X is equal to the Walkway's Height in inches (rounded down). If a Walkway has an Archway beneath it, the area between the Walkway and Archway is treated as Blocking and Climbable Terrain.

Buildings (Flat and Steep)
Buildings are a common feature in Malifaux. Buildings should not be wider than 6″ on any given side (excluding any stairways on their sides).

Flat Buildings have roofs that allow models to stand atop them. These Buildings count as Height X, Blocking, Climbable Terrain, where X is equal to the Building's Height in inches (rounded down to the nearest whole number). Flat Buildings should not be taller than Height 4.

Steep Buildings have roofs that do not allow models to stand atop them. Steep Buildings count as Height X, Blocking, Impassable Terrain, where X is equal to the Building's height in inches (rounded down to the nearest whole number).

ADVANCED BUILDING RULES

When the players are defining terrain, they can declare that one or more of the table's Buildings can be entered.

To enter a Building, a model must be physically able to do so (i.e., it must move through an opening in the wall, such as a doorway or hole, that is large enough for its base to fit). Place effects cannot move a model into or out of a Building.

If any portion of a model's base is within the interior boundaries of a Building, that model is considered to be inside the Building.

Models inside a Building are considered to be entirely within that Building's Shadow. When a model draws LoS to another model on the same floor as a Building they are both in, they ignore that Building and its Shadow (though not any interior walls).

Buildings sometimes have open windows or doors. The portions of a Building's wall immediately above and below an open window or door are not considered to be Blocking Terrain for the purposes of drawing sight lines into and out of (but not through) a Building.

TERRAIN

Fences and Walls
Fences and Walls are both obstructions that prevent movement. Fences do not obstruct LoS and can be easily destroyed, while Walls block LoS and are too sturdy to destroy.

Fences are Height X, Climbable, Destructible Terrain, where X is equal to the Fence's height in inches (rounded down).

Walls are Height X, Blocking, Climbable Terrain, where X is equal to the Wall's height in inches (rounded down).

Fog Bank
Banks of fog are not uncommon in Malifaux, particularly in the early morning or late evening.

Fog Banks are Concealing and Dense.

Hill
Hills are fairly common beyond the walls of Malifaux City, particularly in the appropriate-named Northern Hills.

Models that move horizontally on a Hill do not have to spend any additional movement for changing elevation.

Hills count as Height X Terrain. The Height Trait of a Hill varies depending upon where a model is standing on it; X is equal to the distance between the lowest part of the model's base and the table in inches (rounded down).

Obstacles
Obstacles can be anything from crates to large rocks to stacks of coffins.

Crates count as Height X, Blocking, Climbable, Destructible Terrain, where X is equal to the total Height of the crates in inches (rounded down to the nearest whole number).

If the crates are spread out in a loose line, calculate each area of different Height as a separate terrain piece. If they are bunched together, use the tallest crate to calculate the stack's Height.

Staircase
Staircases allow a model to quickly move up or down the side of a building.

Models that move horizontally along a staircase do not have to spend any additional movement for changing elevation.

Staircases count as Height X, Blocking, Climbable, Terrain. The Height Trait of a Staircase varies depending upon where a model is standing on it; X is equal to the distance between the lowest part of the model's base and the table in inches (rounded down).

Water
Water includes both rivers and ponds.

Water counts as Severe Terrain.

Woods
Patches of woods often include underbrush and one or more trees.

Woods count as Concealing, Dense, Severe Terrain.

ENCOUNTERS

Every game of Malifaux uses the rules for Encounters to set up and play the game. The Encounters detailed in this section are the standard Encounters, but some narrative play (such as campaigns) may modify these standard Encounters.

The rules for Encounters will outline the rules that are needed to set up the game, hire Crews, and determine the winner.

In organized play events, such as tournaments, there may be some variations on these steps, which would be provided in that event's documentation.

Encounters use the following order:

1. **Encounter Set Up**
    - A. Determine Encounter Size
    - B. Place and Define Terrain
    - C. Determine Scenario
    - D. Generate Schemes
    - E. Choose Faction and Leader
    - F. Hire Crew
    - G. Reveal Crews
    - H. Choose Schemes
    - I. Deployment
    - J. Start of Game
2. **Gameplay:** Follow the Turn Sequence on page 56.
3. **End of Encounter:** When the game has ended, determine the winner.

> What you'll find in the Encounter section is just the beginning. Malifaux is a game that will live and breathe for a long time to come.
>
> To make sure that gameplay stays exciting throughout the years, new Strategies, Schemes, and more will be made available for free on our website. Keep an eye out for Story Encounters and Gaining Grounds Season documents for new ways to spice up the game.

ENCOUNTER SETUP

To set up a game, proceed through the ten steps (A through J) as outlined on the next few pages.

A. Determine Encounter Size

Players should agree on the size of the game, which determines the number of points that can be used when hiring.

A standard game is usually 50 Soulstones, but players may choose any value that suits them.

B. Place and Define Terrain

Players should place terrain on the table and then define each terrain piece, with an eye toward having a diverse selection of Terrain Traits (see "Terrain Traits" on pg. 72).

A standard Malifaux table is 3 feet by 3 feet. Roughly a third of its surface should be covered in terrain.

Using the correct amount of terrain and having a variety of represented Terrain Traits is important to ensuring that games of Malifaux are fun for both players. Long-range Actions are intended to be somewhat limited by terrain that offers Concealment and/or Cover. Severe Terrain is intended to shape the game by making some areas of the table more difficult to reach.

Don't worry too much about not having correctly themed terrain for the table. While well-painted, appropriate terrain looks great, players should feel free to use whatever they have on hand to populate the table, such as books, cups, etc.

> ### TALL TERRAIN
>
> In general, it is recommended that any terrain piece that exceeds 4″ in height treats its roof as Impassable.

ENCOUNTERS

C. Determine Scenario

Both players shuffle their Fate Decks and flip the top card off of it, re-flipping any Jokers. The player that flips higher will be the Attacker and the other player will be the Defender; these designations are utilized when determining the setup of an Encounter. The Attacker has Initiative until the Initiative flip of Turn One. If there is a tie, both players reflip.

The suit of the Attacker's card will determine the Strategy that is being used. Each player may score up to a total of 4 Victory Points (**VP**) from the Strategy. The list of Strategies can be found on pages 80 and 81.

The suit of the Defender's card will determine the Deployment Type. The four Deployment Types are listed to the right.

In addition to the distinctions shown on the graphics on this page, there are a few key terms that are necessary to know.

- **Centerpoint:** The exact center of the table.
- **Centerline:** Shown on each deployment type.
- **Table Edge:** Any length of the four 36″ long sides of the table, beyond which models cannot move.
- **Table Half:** The Centerline always bisects the table into two equal halves.
- **Table Corner:** Any place where two table edges meet. There are four table corners.
- **Table Quarter:** An 18″ by 18″ square section of the table. Each table has four table quarters, each of which extends halfway along the table edge from the table corners.
- **Friendly:** When friendly is applied to a physical part of the table, it means the part with your Deployment Zone. For example, a friendly table edge is any table edge touched by your Deployment Zone.
- **Enemy:** When enemy is applied to a physical part of the table, it means the part with your opposing player's Deployment Zone. For example, an enemy table half is the half that includes their Deployment Zone.

Standard Deployment
A player will deploy within 8″ of a chosen table edge, with the opponent deploying within 8″ of the opposite table edge.

Corner Deployment
A player will deploy within 12″ of a chosen table corner, with the opponent deploying within 12″ of the opposite table corner.

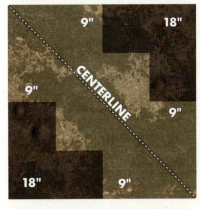

Flank Deployment
The table is divided into four quarters. A player will deploy within 9″ of the table edges within one quarter, with the opponent deploying in the opposite quarter.

Wedge Deployment
A player will deploy in a wedge starting 12″ from the center of the table edge and sweeping back to the corners, with the opponent deploying opposite.

ENCOUNTERS

D. Generate Schemes

Like Strategies, Schemes score Victory Points (VP) that help players win the game. Each game includes a pool of five potential Schemes, from which each player will choose two as their personal Schemes for this Encounter. Schemes are not chosen at this stage, but the players can use the knowledge of which Schemes are available to help them make strategic hiring decisions.

Schemes are worth a total of 2 VP each, for a total of 4 possible VP from both Schemes.

To generate Schemes, the Attacker flips five cards from their Fate Deck to generate the Scheme Pool. The numeric value of the cards determines which Schemes are available to be chosen. Set these cards aside for reference later. At the Start of the game, shuffle these cards back into the Attacker's Fate Deck.

If any duplicates or Jokers are flipped, re-flip them.

The list of Schemes can be found on pages 82 and 83.

E. Choose Faction and Leader

Each player simultaneously chooses a Faction for their Crew and announces it to their opponent. (Dead Man's Hand is not a Faction and cannot be declared as such.)

Once Factions are determined, each player chooses a single Leader from their chosen Faction to command their Crew through the Encounter.

Any Master or Henchman can be chosen as a Leader, but Masters cannot be hired in Crews led by a Henchman Leader.

Once both players have selected their Leader, they reveal the name of their Leader, though not its title, simultaneously.

When hiring Crews, each player must hire their chosen Leader. However, that Leader's Cost is treated as 0 when hiring.

F. Hire Crew

Hiring a Crew consists of selecting models and Upgrades. A player may hire any models that share one or more Keywords with their Leader. The total Cost of all models and Upgrades hired by a player's Crew cannot exceed the game's Encounter Size. Some game effects can affect how a Crew hires models. These game effects are listed as "when hiring" on a model's card.

Additionally, a player may hire any models that belong to their declared Faction, though models that do not share a Keyword with their Crew's Leader have their Cost increased by +1 during hiring. The exception to this rule are models with the Versatile Characteristic, which do not have their Cost increased when they are hired.

By default, you may only hire one copy of a given model into your Crew. Some models, however, have numbers listed after their Station (Master, Henchman, Enforcer, or Minion) Characteristic. If a model lists a number in this way, you may instead hire a number of copies of that model up to the listed value (i.e. model limit).

During hiring, any model can pay for and Attach a single Upgrade. This limit only applies during hiring; there is no limit to the number of Upgrades a model may Attach during gameplay. A Crew can only purchase Upgrades that match its declared Faction.

After hiring your Crew, any unspent points become Soulstones in your Crew's Soulstone Pool. A Crew's Soulstone Pool cannot exceed 10 Soulstones during hiring (but may exceed this limit during gameplay).

> ### TOTEMS
>
> Totems are special models that are intrinsically linked to a Master listed in their Totem Characteristic.
>
> A Totem can only be hired if the linked Master is also in the Crew. If this Master is a Crew's Leader, the Totem's Cost is considered to be 0 during hiring.
>
> During gameplay, a Totem can only be Summoned if the linked Master is still in play and in the Crew.

ENCOUNTERS

G. Reveal Crews

Once both players have finished hiring their Crews, the Crews are revealed to each other. This reveal shows all aspects of the Crew, including the models chosen, their Titles (if any), and any Upgrades.

H. Choose Schemes

With full knowledge of the opponent's Crew, each player secretly selects two Schemes from the Scheme Pool. Schemes are generally written down and kept secret until they begin scoring points, at which point they are revealed as detailed in their individual rules.

Some Schemes may require you to secretly choose a specific model. This choice should be written down for reference during the game, as the chosen model(s) must be revealed when the Scheme is revealed.

I. Deployment

The Attacker chooses a Deployment Zone and divides their Crew into two groups (with any number of models in each group). The Defender chooses one of those two groups, and the Attacker deploys that group within the chosen Deployment Zone.

The Defender then deploys their Crew completely within the opposite Deployment Zone. Finally, the Attacker deploys their remaining group completely within their Deployment Zone.

J. Start of Game

Once the models are deployed, both players shuffle their Fate Decks, including any cards used to determine Strategies and the Scheme Pool. This should leave each player with a full, fresh deck of 54 cards. Each player should give the other player an opportunity to cut their deck.

Now it's the start of the game! Any effects that happen at the start of the game happen now. If multiple effects happen, the player with Initiative may choose the order in which they resolve. The Attacker is always considered to have Initiative until the first Turn's Initiative flip.

GAMEPLAY

Once all start of game effects are complete, players jump into the first Turn (without shuffling), following the structure outlined on page 56.

No player may score VP on the first Turn.

END OF ENCOUNTER

At the end of the Encounter, each player totals up all the VP they've earned. The player with the most VP is the winner.

TITLES

Titles represent different versions of the same character within the Malifaux universe. As such, those characters cannot exist in two time periods at once.

If a Crew contains a model with a Title, it cannot hire any models of the same name that have a different Title. (Models with no Title are treated as having a different Title than models that have a Title.) During gameplay, though they have the same name, models that have different Titles are treated as separate models and can have different model limits, abilities, and other effects.

DEAD MAN'S HAND

A few characters who have left the world of Malifaux (due to death, imprisonment, etc.) still exist in the game in the form of Dead Man's Hand (DMH) models.

Dead Man's Hand models are not traditionally allowed in Tournament or Story play. However, with the event organizer's approval, DMH models may be used as normal models.

Dead Man's Hand is not a Faction and cannot be declared as such.

HAH ... too soon?

STRATEGIES

Below are the four Strategies in the game. Remember, no Victory Points can be scored on the first Turn, and models with the **Insignificant** Ability are ignored for the purposes of Strategies and Schemes in every way.

Turf War

Divide the table into four table quarters. In the center of each table quarter, Drop a neutral Strategy Marker. Drop another neutral Strategy Marker in the center of the table. Strategy Markers are Impassable.

Strategy Markers can be either friendly, neutral, or enemy. A Strategy Marker friendly to one player is enemy to the other (and vice versa). A model can take the **Interact** Action targeting a Strategy Marker in base contact with it to change its alignment from enemy to neutral or from neutral to friendly.

When a friendly model kills an enemy model, it can change one Strategy Marker in the same table quarter as the killed model from enemy to neutral, if possible (the Marker in the center is considered to be in every table quarter).

If a model is in more than one table quarter, the model that killed it may decide which table quarter the killed model was in.

At the end of each Turn, a Crew gains 1 **VP** if it has more friendly Strategy Markers than it has scored **VP** for this Strategy.

Plant Explosives

After Deployment, starting with the player with Initiative, each player alternates placing Explosives Tokens on their deployed models until each player has placed a total of five Explosives Tokens on their models.

Minions can have a maximum of one Explosive Token placed on them, while non-Minions can have a maximum of two Explosives Tokens placed on them.

A model with one or more Explosives Tokens can take the **Interact** Action to discard an Explosives Token and Drop a Strategy Marker into base contact with itself. Strategy Markers cannot be Dropped within 6″ of another friendly Strategy Marker.

A model in base contact with a Strategy Marker can take the **Interact** Action to discard the Strategy Marker and gain an Explosives Token.

If a model with one or more Explosives Tokens is killed, a model in the opposing Crew that is within 3″ of the killed model may gain the killed model's Explosives Tokens. Otherwise, they are discarded.

At the end of each Turn, a Crew gains 1 **VP** if there are more Strategy Markers on the opponent's table half than this Crew has earned **VP** from this Strategy. Strategy Markers on the centerline count as being in both table halves.

STRATEGIES

Corrupted Idols (♥)

At the start of each Turn, after determining which player has Initiative, Drop a Strategy Marker centered on the centerline. The location of the Strategy Marker is determined by the suit of the Initiative Flip of the player with Initiative (and the direction is calculated from that player's perspective):

- ♥: 8″ from where the centerline meets the table edge on the left.
- 📖: 8″ from where the centerline meets the table edge on the right.
- 🌀: On the centerpoint.
- ✗: Where the centerline meets the table edge (player with Initiative chooses which table edge).
- **Joker**: Reflip.

If the Strategy Marker would be Dropped on top of a Strategy Marker, Impassable Terrain, or a model, the player with Initiative instead Drops the Strategy Marker evenly on the centerline, touching but not overlapping that Strategy Marker, Impassable Terrain, or model. If this is not possible, the Strategy Marker is not Dropped.

A model in base contact with a Strategy Marker can take the **Interact** Action and suffer up to three irreducible damage, ignoring **Hard to Kill**. A model may not suffer more damage than its current Health.

Drop the Strategy Marker anywhere within X″ of its current location, not into base contact with a model or Impassable Terrain, where X is equal to the amount of damage suffered by the Interacting model (even if it was killed by the damage it suffered).

At the end of each Turn, a Crew gains 1 **VP** if there are more Strategy Markers completely on the opponent's table half than it has earned **VP** from this Strategy.

Reckoning (✗)

At the end of each Turn, a Crew gains 1 **VP** if more enemy models were killed that Turn than it has scored **VP** for this Strategy, or if there are no more enemy models in play.

For the purposes of this Strategy, enemy Leaders and Masters each count as three models when killed and enemy Henchmen each count as two models when killed.

CORE RULEBOOK • MALIFAUX THIRD EDITION

SCHEMES

Each Scheme can be scored twice per game: once for its "Reveal" requirement and once for its "End" requirement. The "End" requirement of a Scheme typically can be scored even if a player did not score its "Reveal" requirement (and vice versa).

A Scheme cannot grant more than one **VP** per Turn.

If a Scheme requires a player to secretly choose a specific model, that model must be in the appropriate Crew when the Scheme is selected. "Enemy" and "Friendly" are from the point of view of the Scheming Crew. Remember, no Victory Points can be scored on the first Turn, and models with the **Insignificant** Ability are ignored for the purposes of Strategies and Schemes.

1. Detonate Charges

Reveal: At the end of the Turn, if you have two or more friendly Scheme Markers within 2″ of the same enemy model, you may reveal this Scheme and remove two such Scheme Markers to gain 1 **VP**.

End: At the end of the game, if you have two or more friendly Scheme Markers within 2″ of the same enemy model, you may remove two such Scheme Markers to gain 1 **VP**.

2. Breakthrough

Reveal: At the end of the Turn, if you have one or more friendly Scheme Markers and a friendly model in the enemy Deployment Zone, and there are no enemy models within 3″ of that model, you may reveal this Scheme and remove one such Scheme Marker to gain 1 **VP**.

End: At the end of the game, if you have three or more friendly Scheme Markers in the enemy Deployment Zone, you may remove three such Scheme Markers to gain 1 **VP**.

3. Harness the Ley Line

Reveal: At the end of the Turn, if you have three or more friendly Scheme Markers on the centerline, you may reveal this Scheme and remove three such Scheme Markers to gain 1 **VP**.

End: At the end of the game, if you have three or more friendly Scheme Markers on the centerline, you may remove three such Scheme Markers to gain 1 **VP**.

4. Search the Ruins

Reveal: At the end of the Turn, if you have two or more friendly Scheme Markers on the opponent's table half, each in base contact with a different piece of terrain, you may reveal this Scheme and remove two such Scheme Markers to gain 1 **VP**.

End: At the end of the game, if you have three or more different friendly Scheme Markers on the opponent's table half, each in base contact with a different piece of terrain, you may remove three such Scheme Markers to gain 1 **VP**.

5. Dig Their Graves

Reveal: After killing an enemy model within 1″ of one or more friendly Scheme Markers, you may reveal this Scheme and remove one such Scheme Marker to gain 1 **VP**.

End: At the end of the game, if you have three or more different Scheme Markers within 1″ of three different Corpse or Scrap Markers, you may remove three such Scheme Markers to gain 1 **VP**.

6. Hold Up Their Forces

Reveal: At the end of the Turn, if you have two or more friendly models, each engaging a different enemy model with higher Cost than itself, you may reveal this Scheme to gain 1 **VP**.

End: At the end of the game, if you have two or more friendly models, each engaging a different enemy model with higher Cost than itself, gain 1 **VP**.

7. Take Prisoner

At the beginning of the game, secretly choose an enemy Minion or Enforcer.

Reveal: At the end of the Turn, if you have a friendly model engaging the secretly chosen model and there are no other enemy models within 4″ of the secretly chosen model, you may reveal this Scheme to gain 1 **VP**.

End: At the end of the game, if you have a friendly model engaging the secretly chosen model, or after this Scheme was revealed, if the secretly chosen model was killed by a model which was friendly to it, gain 1 **VP**.

SCHEMES

8. Power Ritual

Reveal: At the end of the Turn, if you have a friendly Scheme Marker within 3″ of a table corner not part of your Deployment Zone, you may reveal this Scheme and remove that Scheme Marker to gain 1 **VP**.

End: At the end of the game, if you have three or more different friendly Scheme Markers within 3″ of three different table corners, with no more than one table corner as part of your Deployment Zone, you may remove those Scheme Markers to gain 1 **VP**.

9. Outflank

Reveal: At the end of the Turn, if you have two models, each within 3″ of where the centerline meets a different table edge or corner, you may reveal this Scheme to gain 1 **VP**.

End: At the end of the game, if you have two models, each within 3″ of where the centerline meets a different table edge or corner, gain 1 **VP**.

10. Assassinate

Reveal: At the end of the Turn, if the enemy Leader is in play and has half its maximum Health or less, you may reveal this Scheme to gain 1 **VP**.

End: At the end of the game, if the enemy Leader is not in play, gain 1 **VP**.

11. Deliver a Message

At the beginning of the game, secretly choose an enemy Leader or Master.

Reveal: During its Activation, a friendly model within 1″ of the secretly chosen model can take the **Interact** Action to target the secretly chosen model (the secretly chosen model is not treated as engaging the friendly model for the purposes of this **Interact** Action). If it does so, you may reveal this Scheme to gain 1 **VP**.

End: At the end of the game, if the secretly chosen model is still in play and within 2″ of a friendly Scheme Marker, or after this Scheme was revealed, if the secretly chosen model was killed by a model which was friendly to it, gain 1 **VP**.

12. Claim Jump

At the beginning of the game, secretly choose a friendly non-Leader model.

Reveal: At the end of the Turn, if there are no enemy models within 3″ of the secretly chosen model and the secretly chosen model is within 2″ of the centerpoint, you may reveal this Scheme to gain 1 **VP**.

End: At the end of the game, if the secretly chosen model is still in play with half or more of its maximum Health and within 2″ of the centerpoint, gain 1 **VP**.

13. Vendetta

At the beginning of the game, secretly choose a friendly non-Totem model and an enemy non-Leader model with higher Cost.

Reveal: At the end of the friendly model's Activation, if it successfully dealt damage to the secretly chosen enemy model and the enemy model has half its maximum Health or less (but is still in play), you may reveal this Scheme to gain 1 **VP**.

End: At the end of the game, if the friendly model is in play and the enemy model is not, gain 1 **VP**.

INDEX

A

Abilities 40, 41, 60
Accuracy Fate Modifier 60
Actions 40, 41, 48, 58, 59
Action Limit 57, 70
Activation Phase 57
Active Player 46, 57
Adversary 65
Assassinate 83
Assist 58, 65
Attach 42, 78
Attack Actions 58
Auras 58, 66
Away 51

B

Base Contact 49, 50
Bases 40, 49
Base Size 40, 41, 64
Blasts 66
Blocked LoS 52, 54
Blocking (terrain) 73
Bonus Action 48, 58
Breakthrough 82
Burning 65
Bury 69

C

Centerline 77
Centerpoint 77
Chain Activations 57
Characteristics 40, 41, 61
Charge 58
Cheating Fate 45, 46
Claim Jump 83
Climbable 50, 72, 73
Concealment 72
Concealing (terrain) 73
Concentrate 58
Conditions 65
Conflict 44
Construct 61
Control 62
Control Hand 43
Corner (table) 77
Corpse Marker 61
Corrupted Idols 81
Cost (effect) 48, 58, 59
Cost (stat) 40, 41, 42, 78
Cover 54, 72
Create 64
Crew 39, 62, 78, 79

D

Damage 60, 63, 69, 70
Damage Flips 60
Damage Reduction 60
Dead Man's Hand 79
Declaring Actions 59, 62
Declaring Triggers 47, 48, 59
Defense (Df) 40
Deliver a Message 83
Dense (terrain) 53, 73
Deployment 77, 79
Destructible 73
Detailed Timing 71
Detonate Charges 82
Dig Their Graves 82
Discard Pile 44
Disengage 58
Distracted 65
Draw 43, 56, 63
Drop 64
Duel 46, 47, 59, 63

E

Edge (table) 77
Encounters 39, 76
End of Game 57
End Phase 57
Enemy 62, 77
Engagement 62

F

Faction 40, 41, 78
Faction (symbol) 2, 3
Fast 57, 65
Fate Card 43, 44, 46
Fate Deck 38, 39, 43, 44
Fate Modifier 45, 46, 60
Final Duel Total 46, 47
Flips 44
Focused 58, 65
Friendly 62, 77
Friendly Fire 62

G

Gameplay 56
General Actions 58
Generated Actions 48, 70

H

Half (table) 77
Harness the Ley Line 82
Hazardous (terrain) 72, 73
Healing 61
Health 40, 41
Height 49, 54, 73
Hire Crew 78
Hold Up Their Forces 82

I

Impassable (terrain) 72, 73
Initiative 56, 70, 79
Injured 65
Interact 58, 62, 68

J

Jokers 43, 45

K

Keyword 40, 41, 78
Killed 61

L

Leader 57, 78
Limitations 42
Line of Sight (LoS) 52
Living 61

M

Markers 61, 62, 64, 72
Maximum Hand Size 43, 56
Measuring 49
Melee 58, 62
Model 38, 40, 45
Model Limits 68
Moderate 43, 44, 60
Move 50
Movement (Mv) 40

O

Once Per 69
Opposed Duel 46
Outflank 83

INDEX

P
Pass 56, 57, 68, 71
Phases 56, 57
Place 50, 51
Plant Explosives 80
Plentiful 42
Poison 65
Power Ritual 83
Projectile 58, 62
Pulse 58, 67
Push 50, 51

Q
Quarter (table) 77

R
Range 49, 58, 59
Reckoning 81
Relenting (Duels) 46
Removed From the Game 43
Replace 68
Resistance Triggers 48
Resolving Actions 59
Revealing Cards 44
Rule of Intent 69

S
Scheme Marker 58, 64
Schemes 57, 71, 78, 79, 82, 83
Scrap Marker 61
Search the Ruins 82
Severe (terrain) 73
Severe (variable) 43, 44, 60
Shadow 54, 73
Shielded 65
Shockwaves 67
Sight Lines 52, 55
Simple Duel 46
Simultaneous Effects 70
Size (Sz) 40
Slow 57, 65
Soulstones 39, 63, 76, 78
Special Restrictions 48, 59
Staggered 65
Start Phase 56
Stat Card 40, 41
Stats 40, 41
Strategies 80, 81
Strategy Marker 64
Stunned 57, 65
Success 47, 48, 59
Suits 43
Summoning 68

T
Table 49, 77
Tactical Actions 58
Take Prisoner 82
Tape Measure 38
Target 59
Terrain 38, 72
Timing 48, 70
Title 40, 41, 79
Tokens 63
Totem 78
Toward 51
Triggers 47, 48
Trigger Timing 48
Turf War 80
Turn Sequence 56

U
Upgrades 42, 68, 78
Undead 61

V
Variable Profiles 44
Vendetta 83
Versatile 78
Victory Points (VP) 57, 77, 80, 82

W
Walk 50, 58, 62
Weak 43, 44, 60, 66
Willpower (Wp) 40
Winning the Game 57

X
"X" Variable 44

ICONOGRAPHY

Positive Fate Modifier:
Negative Fate Modifer:
Melee (Action):
Projectile (Action):
Bonus Action:
Blast:
Pulse:
Aura:

Suits
Crow: Mask:
Ram: Tome:

Continue to Explore The World of Malifaux

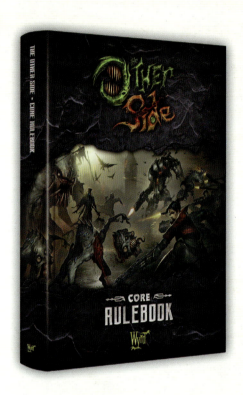

The mysterious Burning Man has opened portals linking Earth to Malifaux and flooded the world with monstrous hordes and insidious cults. Will you join their ranks, or will you fight back against the invaders by taking command of Earth's strongest nations?

The Other Side is a battlefield-scale miniatures wargame that leaves the fate of Earth in the hands of the players.

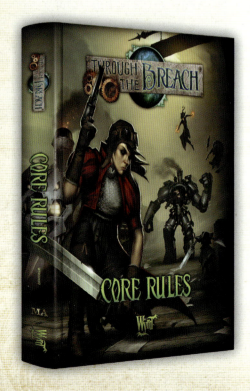

A tabletop roleplaying game set in the world of Malifaux, Through the Breach lets players create their own characters to explore the complex and dangerous world of Malifaux. The hand of fate is cruel, however, and each character will eventually have to confront their terrible destiny…